Who Cares

Joe Welsh

Published in 2016 by FeedARead.com Publishing

A CIP catalogue record for this title is available from the British Librar

Every Child Matters: The Five identified outcomes.

1). Be healthy.

2). Stay Safe.

3). Enjoy and Achieve.

4). Make a Positive Contribution.

5). Achieve Economic Well-being.

***

This book is a work of fiction. The names, characters and incidents portrayed are the work of the author's imagination.

***

DEDICATED

To the memory of John Gardiner 1936 –2007
Who told me: 'Whatever you do, find a way
that you can still be creative.'

For My Wife, Karin
Your love sustains me
You set my spirit free

For my nephew, Philip
There are no words for the kindness
And love you have shown

Book One

Charlie's Story

The hero of my tale–whom I love
with all the power of my soul,
whom I have tried to portray
in all his beauty, who has
been, and is, and will be beautiful– is truth.
(Leo Tolstoy)

Chapter one

I arrived at seven-thirty in the morning. The place itself was unimpressive. The building stood back from the other houses, its plain grey walls at odds with their red bricks and washing lines. On the ground floor, to the right, one large window dominated. It needed cleaning. The top half of the dwelling was made up of a dark wood that in places had begun to rot. An old shoe rested in the guttering, an aerial wire flapped in the breeze. A few crisp packets and plastic water cups were scattered across the small lawn, trodden cigarette butts littered the front step.

I was met out front by a polite, softly spoken lady. She had a mop of peroxide hair with a pair of half-cocked glasses sitting on top.

'Hi, you must be Jerry. I'm Shelly, the team leader for today.'

She looked tired as if the coffee she was sipping hadn't yet hit its mark.

'Nice to meet you,' I said, shaking her hand.

'Welcome to the mad house,' she said, yawning. 'Excuse me. Would you like a drink?'

'No thanks I'm fine.'

I entered the hall; stairs faced me directly. A painting of flowers on the wall emblazoned with vibrant colours proclaimed: ***Welcome to Acorn House.*** There were other framed pictures of pebbles, footprints in the sand and dolphins somersaulting above blue waves. The hall was partly furnished with what looked like a Formica cupboard, its only ornament a lamp with its shade bent out of shape on one side, which someone had forgotten to turn off. There was a hole in the plaster wall the size of a tennis ball just behind the lamp. The walls were painted a dull yellow with the paint flaking in places.

There were three kids up and about. I guessed their ages to be somewhere between twelve and sixteen. The boys huddled together on the stairs, sleepy eyed. They looked at odds with the early morning. 'This is Jerry–'Shelly said. 'He's come to work with us.' The kids looked me over, smiling first at me and then to each other. I returned the smiles and nodded a firm hello, hoping I'd met with their approval. 'The other four are still in the land of nod but they'll be up later,' said Shelly.

A heavy set woman with a round welcoming face came coughing down the stairs carrying a vacuum cleaner. She wore grey tracksuit bottoms speckled with dried white paint.

'Debbie, this is, Jerry, our new relief worker,' said Shelly. 'Debbie's our night worker.'

'Hi,' said Debbie, blowing out her cheeks and giving a quick wave of her hand before locking the vacuum into a walk-in cupboard.

It was pocket money day. Shelly asked if I would like to accompany the boys to the local shop. I agreed, hoping I sounded more confident than I felt.

*

At thirty-four I had gained a degree in Sociology. If nothing else my educational journey had shone a light on the injustices in the world and while I had no fixed idea what I wanted to do, I always had the desire to do something positive, something that made a difference but I didn't know what. I ended up working for ASDA on the late shift in a warehouse and I hated it, but it was the only job I could get.

A friend of mine suggested going on a relief bank of workers to work with kids in Local Authority Care. She'd done it, briefly, to gain experience. She said at times the behaviour of the children could be difficult but on the whole she'd found it very rewarding. She'd travelled round working in a few children's homes getting the odd shift here and there before securing a full-time job as a learning mentor at a local college. Anyway, she reckoned I would be good at it, enjoy it and make a little money at the same time.

The thought of all those children from abused backgrounds made me feel very sad so I was more than happy to jump in and do something worthwhile. My wife, Kate, was working part-time at a travel agency and Millie; our daughter had just turned seven.

A month or so later I was called to interview. A middle-aged man and woman sat across from me at a small table in a room so well lit I could see the faint growth of hair on the woman's upper lip.

It was the man who asked the majority of questions while the woman observed, interjecting when she felt my answers needed to be expanded . I paced my replies, taking sips of water from my polystyrene cup, occasionally shifting my position in the uncomfortable blue plastic chair. I rattled off that I realised as a reformed young tear-away I now knew that this, on reflection, had been part of the normal transition to the responsible adult you now see before you. I now wished to be an advocate (a buzz word I was advised to drop in by my friend but it *was true*, I wanted to help) for children and young people. I got the job. Three weeks later I started work.

***

Chapter 2

Three months into the job I met Charlie. He was fifteen-years-old. His hair was a dirty blond, short-cropped, and his eyes were a deep sad blue. Charlie had been placed in local authority care due to an adoption breakdown. At the age of fifteen, like many other fifteen-year-olds, he'd begun staying out late, and on the odd occasion getting drunk. He also argued with his father and at one point threatened to hit him. He was, his father said, becoming a problem to the harmony of the family, drinking and refusing to accept any boundaries. He was also worried about the affect it was having on Charlie's twelve-year-old sister, Amanda. Charlie and Amanda had been adopted together.

It all came to a head one night when Charlie came home after his curfew, climbed through a back window and in the process trampled his Dad's prize strawberries.

The next day, after things had calmed down, Charlie said he no longer wished to live with his adoptive parents and Social Services were contacted in an effort to find a way forward. His parents dropped him off at Acorn House one Friday evening with an overnight bag for what was to be a short period of respite for Charlie and his family.

Charlie was admitted into the emergency bed. This would be, as policy dictated, for a seventy-two hour period.

As a relief worker I held little responsibility other than hanging out with the kids, no monthly summaries to write, no key child, just the client diaries to fill out at the end of each shift. Here one would just give a basic overview of the children's day: did they attend school, were they well behaved and did they settle well at bed time?

Charlie and I hit it off right away. I felt sorry for him. As a teenager I had had a fragile relationship with my parents and I guess I saw a little of myself in him. Over the next few days I got to know Charlie a bit and would drive him to the station so he could catch the train for school. He was no trouble, always polite and kind.

'See yer later Jerry lad, have a good one.'

'Yeah, you too Charlie, catch you later.' And with that he would be off quickly moving en masse with the other kids, lost in a sea of school uniforms.

*

One night Charlie showed me his life story: this was a book that had been put together by his former social worker and consisted of a compilation of photographs of Charlie and his sister when they were little. I told Charlie I thought Amanda was a sweet name.

There was no mention of his birth father and when I asked, Charlie simply said, 'I don't know anything about my dad.' Something in the tone of his voice told me not to push the subject.

There was one picture that Charlie stopped at longer than any of the others.

'This is my mum, Pat,' he said. 'I never knew her.' The picture showed a slender young woman, sitting in an armchair, her shoes kicked off and her legs folded under her. She was smiling into the camera; I wondered if Charlie's father had taken the picture.

'We were taken off her when I was four and Amanda was one because she couldn't cope.' He breathed in sharply. 'It's what she wanted. She wanted us to have a better life,' and then he said, 'I hope to find her one day.' I didn't have the words to say anything, so instead, I let the silence hang before asking if he had any hobbies.

'I've got medals for swimming,' he said. I could tell that this was a bright kid, of good upbringing. Both his adoptive parents were professional people. His adoptive father was a police officer and his adoptive mother a paralegal. I was a little shocked when I heard this but I guess even well-educated people don't have all the answers when it comes to bringing up children.

*

I grew up on a council estate, its dull grey houses squashed together like headstones. Flat unimaginative architecture dominated the landscape in every direction. Faded plastic drainpipes linked the houses together like the hardened arteries of a decaying body.

I crashed out of school like a freedom call. I never liked school. I'd not been a bad kid but I never did my homework and found learning difficult. It was easier to fool about in the classroom than knuckle down. Around the estate I indulged in the occasional bit of trouble, nothing serious, knock and run and smashing the windows of empty houses before the council boarded them up. There was not much else to do. Mostly, we used our imaginations and turned our concrete jungle into an adventure forest of invading soldiers or a marching army of super villains.

My relationship with my father had not been a loving one. I mean I loved him and in his own way he may have loved me but it was never expressed. He never came right out and said: 'Jerry boy, I love you.' Conversations, on the odd occasion he was on a shift that allowed him to eat his evening meal with us, would be basic.

'You okay?'

'Yeah, you okay Pop?'

'Not bad. Not bad.'

Then his handkerchief would come out of his pocket, wiping the grease from his mouth and stretching out his arms he'd sit back behind his newspaper. I put it down to me being the eldest. My sister, Brenda, being four years younger than me was the centre of Mum and Dad's world. With Dad working long hours at the plastic factory and Mum looking after the home and my sister, perhaps there simply wasn't enough time for me.

I often watched Dad from my bedroom window, shuffling across the field towards work, his head bowed as he walked. I knew when my time came I wanted to do a job that made the world a better place. What the job would be I didn't know but I couldn't allow myself to become my father. I certainly, at that time, had no educational aspirations. Mum said many times, 'Education is a waste of time. Getting a job is what matters.'

My Dad made no comment except when he was sure Mum had left the room, 'You're only young once lad so spread your wings,' after which he climbed back into his newspaper. It was the only advice he ever gave me.

At sixteen I spent three months on a government training scheme learning how to weld but got sacked. Monday morning the supervisor had lined us all up to give us feedback on our training so far. When he finished he asked if there was any questions.

I put up my hand.

'Yes?' he said abruptly.

'Who won the FA Cup in 1945?' I asked. The room exploded into laughter and I was dismissed on the spot.

A mate of mine, Jimmy Carol, enrolled at the local college. At first I only went along because Jimmy said there were loads of girls. Basic Maths and English were my starting point in education. College was different than school, more relaxed. The teachers were different too, patient if you didn't understand or get something right the first time. After my year of college I drifted from job to dead end job. Nothing seemed to fit. I didn't fit, until I met Kate. It was only with Kate's encouragement that I returned to education and completed a degree.

*

Kate was twenty-one when I met her, bubbly as a sink full of soap suds. She had smooth child-like features and long dark eye lashes, delicate as newly spun spider's web. Her dark hair tucked behind her ears would slip forward when she moved, the ends just touching the corner of her mouth.

Saturdays we often headed for the funfair in Blackpool, Kate loved the ghost train. Later, at midnight, we would walk along the beach eating fish and chips.

Within two years Kate fell pregnant. Towards the end of the pregnancy she became unwell: high blood pressure resulted in her being hospitalised with complete bed rest. Like most expectant couples our anxiety levels increased. I told Kate not to worry that everything would work out just fine but deep inside I knew something was wrong. Born by caesarean section, six-pounds three ounces, Millie was to be our first and last.

Kate had suffered a prolapse of the uterus and a hysterectomy was the sad but inevitable solution. The news shattered us. Kate wept when the doctor told her she could never have another child.

The day before Kate left the hospital the doctor came to the ward and spoke to us.

'These things happen,' he said, his voice gentle and sympathetic. 'These things are unforeseen.' His tongue floated around his mouth as if looking for the right word, as if it was somewhere in the cavity of his mouth waiting to be located, then scooped up and spoken. 'Take strength in your daughter and the fact you're young enough to adapt.' He paused for a moment to adjust the nose piece on his glasses and rubbed his eyes before replacing his spectacles. He laid a gentle hand onto Kate's arm. 'We have a counsellor attached to the hospital we can put you in touch with if there's anything you think you may like to discuss.'

I remember the next day outside the sun was shining. A couple across the street came out of a chip shop laughing, the man pulling the girl close, his arm around her waist. He pinched a chip, taking half a bite and then playfully feeding the remaining half to the girl.

'Fish and chips?' I said.

'No,' said Kate. 'Not today.'

*

I entered the house to the smell of fresh pine and the sight of sparkling kitchen tiles. I did giant moon leaps across the floor looking back to see a collection of smudged footprints pointing the way to where I was now standing.

Kate's hair was tied up in a bun. Fine beads of perspiration on her forehead shone in the light. She was laughing, joyful as a child. She made a move as if to throw the dishcloth she was holding at me, saw me flinch and laughed. I moved towards her and caught her in an embrace.

'The floor could do with a mop,' I said, squeezing her tight, as she tried to free her arms to give me a playful slap. She gave up and instead planted a kiss on my lips.

'I always knew you were trouble,' she said.

Millie was nibbling away on a piece of sweet corn, end to end, like a human typewriter, her legs dangling above the newly cleaned floor while Kate pretended to sprinkle salt onto her potatoes.

'Mother is coming for tea next Saturday,' said Kate, carefully covering Millie's potatoes in gravy, before placing the jug down. Millie made a grab for it.

'Now Millie be careful you don't put too much on.'

I liked Kate's mother. She only visited us every so often and she never interfered. She had squashed all my preconceived ideas about monster mothers-in-law. Kate's father died when she was eleven and Kate had a strong bond with her mother.

'That's good,' I said, watching Millie chase a pea onto her fork, 'but you do know I'm on a late next Saturday?'

'I do now,' Kate said, smiling.

'Yeah, well I figure make hay whilst the sun shines.'

Kate turned her attention back to Millie. 'Don't shove it all in your mouth. Chew it first like a good girl.'

I continued, 'There's this great kid, Charlie.'

'Charlie?'

'Yeah, Charlie, good kid, sharp, I really feel sorry for him.'

'How long will he be in the home for?'

'I don't know. Not too long I hope. You see the sister is still at home and–'

'What's his sister's name, Daddy?' I looked over at Millie, who had stopped shovelling food into her mouth, an enquiring look on her face.

'His sister's name is Amanda,' I said.

'How old is she?' Millie asked.

'I don't know nosey, about thirteen or fourteen. Just eat your tea.'

Millie smiled, once more tucking into her food.

I turned back to Kate. 'I think it's just a few adolescent pains. You know all the things kids do as they get older. They're trying to teach him a lesson I think. I don't know if putting a kid in care is the answer though.'

'They will take him back won't they?'

'I hope so, Kate.'

'What will happen if they don't, where will he go?'

'I guess he'll stay unless they can foster him but he's too old for that. People tend to want the little cute ones.'

'He could live with us, we've got lots of room,' said Millie, excitement in her voice.

'We've got enough trouble with you,' I said, playfully ruffling her hair.

***

Chapter 3

Saturday was pocket-money day. The kids would rush around making sure their rooms were tidy. For eleven to fifteen-year-olds pocket money was £10.00 per week and £20.00 for sixteen-year-olds. I have to admit when I first heard this I was in shock. As a kid I'd done a paper round in the dead of winter and didn't make as much money.

In my early days at the home it was Alan who educated me about the workings of the pocket money system. He had a face that always looked serious, as if to smile would cause him pain. When he spoke, his glasses slid down his nose and he would push them back up using his forefinger. He was tall, with imposing shoulders, erect like a soldier on parade. He was born an adult. When he spoke he sounded like a human text book.

'The Children's Act states the children must have pocket money each week.'

'Do they have to do chores for their pocket money?' I asked.

'Yes. They must tidy their rooms.'

Alan crossed over to the desk and handed me a large red file with 'Pocket Monies' printed on the side in bold black capitals.

'If you look in here you'll see a pocket money sheet for each child,' he said, flicking the pages. 'If a child's behaviour is inappropriate then you can deduct a pound or fifty pence from their pocket money.'

This seemed absolutely fair to me. I could see this was a method of instilling some sense of boundaries for the children and to my mind all children needed some form of boundary.

Alan replaced the file on the shelf. Pushing his glasses up his nose he continued, 'The money taken for any indiscretions is then placed in the young person's savings, which they can later access and spend with their key worker.'

'Yeah, but if they get it back aren't they just being rewarded for bad behaviour?'

'It's the Children's Act. We're not allowed to punish only to use sanctions to improve behaviour. That way every day is a fresh start.'

I had to admit it was a noble approach and one I could see the merits of but so far the results did not seem to support the theory. Only the day before, one of the kids had told Mavis, a residential child care worker, to fuck off, simply because she asked him to turn the volume on the television down. When he was told using such language would cost him 50 pence, he'd replied, 'Take a fucking quid.'

'Does it work?'

'Not really but it's the rules.'

'Then what's the point?'

'To empower children in the decisions they make.'

An uncomfortable silence followed. I felt it would have been futile to carry the debate with Alan any further and so changed tack.

'Got any kids yourself?'

'That's not important to the job,' he snapped. This dickhead was touchy. I tried again.

'No... of course not, I just meant have you got any kids yourself?'

Alan pushed his glasses up onto his face.

'Yes, a boy, he's twelve and lives with his mother.' *Surprise, surprise* I thought.

As I drove home that night I pushed the conversation with Alan to the back of my mind. 50 pence, a pound, was it really that important? I found the drive home peaceful. Most of the houses I passed were in darkness. I passed a brightly lit petrol station and in the window I could see the solitary figure of the cashier. It all looked so calm and stress free, no bother just the occasional car filling up..

*

It was clear to me from my first week that Alan didn't like me. It got worse when Charlie was admitted. I tried to put myself in Alan's place. Perhaps he felt threatened because although he'd been allocated as Charlie's key worker, they had no relationship that I could see. Charlie certainly appeared to respond in a more positive manner towards me. Alan knew this, as did most of the staff. I think it was my sense of humour that got me off to a good start, not just with Charlie, but with all the kids.

Alan was standing between the gap of a half open kitchen door, one hand on the door handle and his other hand holding the walk-around-phone.

'Just let me get my own crisps,' said Charlie.

'You know you're not allowed in the kitchen. Tell me what flavour you want and I'll get them for you,' said Alan.

'I don't know,' said Charlie in a how-many-times-do-I-have-to-tel- you voice. That's why I wanner look, doh!'

The kitchen door was always locked due to it being an industrial kitchen and the fact the kids would take anything that wasn't nailed down.

'I've told you what's available,' said Alan.

'I have informed you what flavours are available,' Charlie repeated in a robotic voice before bursting into laughter.

Charlie had his hand on the handle and was attempting to pull the door further open but Alan was firmly wedged in the gap. Little Sammy had strolled up and was enjoying the entertainment, a big smile spread across his shiny face.

'Other staff let us in,' said little Sammy.

Alan shot me a look. I had, from time to time, let the kids in the kitchen, and it was true the kids would take advantage and steal food when your back was turned, but I figured they were only stealing off themselves.

'Who let you in?' Alan asked, but Charlie and little Sammy were having none of Alan's little game, Charlie let go of the handle.

'Yer a fucking Muppet,' shouted Charlie.

'Can you not swear at me please?'

The phone interrupted any prospect of an answer from Charlie.

'Hello, Acorn House, Alan speaking.' There was a pause. We all strained to listen before Alan replied, 'Yes he's here…I'll tell him. What's your ETA?' There was another slight pause, which I figured was the person on the other end, asking 'what?'

'Estimated time of arrival. Okay… Thank you, goodbye.' Alan hung up and turned to little

Sammy. 'Sammy your social worker will be here at approximately five o' clock to visit you today.'

'What for?'

'Statutory visit. It's important.'

Little Sammy shrugged his shoulders, 'Who cares?'

'You should, it's for you. In case there's something you're not happy about, then you can sit down and discuss it with your social worker,' said Alan.

'Yeah, like how shit she is,' Sammy giggled. 'Can you get me a glass of milk please?'

I figured little Sammy was attempting to get Alan to move away from the door and so I took the opportunity to step in and try to loosen the tension.

'It's okay Alan. I'll sort Sammy's drink out.' I headed for the other side door that led into the kitchen.

'Jerry lad, get us a packet of crisps while yer there, Salt and Vinegar!' Charlie shouted after me.

I turned to reply and whilst Charlie and little Sammy were preoccupied by me, Alan took the chance to come out of the kitchen, closing the door behind him. Charlie made a momentary dash to catch the closing door, but wasn't quick enough and the lock clicked into place.

'Ah yer… BFG.'

'BFG?' asked Alan.

'Big four-eyed giant,' said Charlie in reply.

'More like BFC,' said little Sammy. Sammy and Charlie looked at each other smiling before simultaneously saying, 'Big four-eyed cunt.'

Both Charlie and little Sammy then began shouting at the top of their voices 'Big four-eyed cunt!' as they marched away up the stairs.

Alan looked at me accusingly, as if I had had some part in it all. As if it was my fault none of the name calling had been directed at me.

'Big four-eyed cunt!'

'Big four-eyed cunt!' Little Sammy stopped half-way up the stairs and did a little jig egged on by Charlie's laughter and applause; taking a bow before finally going upstairs.

*

Little Sammy was twelve and the eldest of four brothers. He had the roundest head I'd ever seen and his brown hair never seemed to grow, as if someone cut it short and it just gave up growing. His two brothers still lived with the mother. 'Immaculate house,' said the social workers who'd been there. All Sammy's reviews were held at home, as Sammy's mother couldn't possibly attend a meeting at Acorn House, as she could never find a babysitter or so she said.

I sat lazily flicking through little Sammy's file. I couldn't find much on little Sammy's father apart from a name. Alan was going over the pocket money file, punching numbers into a calculator. The kids had all gone out to the local shop where they would wait until they could get an adult to go in and buy them cigarettes.

'Does little Sammy have any contact with his dad?' I asked.

Alan looked up.

'The father split with the mother when Sammy was two and hasn't been seen since. His three siblings are the result of three different relationships the mother's had.' Alan tapped the calculator, picked up his pen and wrote the result down. 'But that's not the shocking bit. Sammy's mother told him his father had been mentally sick and she tells Sammy that he's mental just like his father.'

'Is he?'

Alan pushed his glasses up his nose. 'It's best you read his entire file. There have been a number of psychological assessments done on Sammy but they all say he's fine. It's thought the mother lied about the father to add substance to her own argument. You know,' he sat back, 'that Sammy has,' Alan raised his hands and made speech marks in the air, 'a mental condition like his father.' Alan let out a squeak of a laugh. I watched as Alan steadied himself, straightened up cutting his laughter off, tucking it away before it took full flight. 'Of course that's not to say Sammy hasn't got problems.'

'So why was he taken into care?'

'The mother said he was aggressive, constantly fighting with his siblings. Kicking, punching and spitting at them. He also has a tendency to masturbate whenever and wherever the urge strikes him.'

'He's not the only one,' I said.

Alan didn't laugh.

'There was one time he climbed upon the roof in the middle of the night, waking up the whole unit, refusing to come down. When the police came he said Satan told him to do it.'

The phone rang.

'Hello Acorn House, you're speaking to Alan.' Alan scanned the desk for his pen. 'I see. Thank you.' Alan reached for the pocket monies file. 'Speak of the devil. Sammy didn't turn up at his placement earlier today. That's two pounds out of his pocket money this week.'

I thought I saw just a glint of pleasure on Alan's face as he scribbled on the file before he placed it back on the shelf.

'Does he still see his mother?'

'He did but only at weekends.'

'Did?'

'The problem was… is,' said Alan as he removed his glasses and scratched his nose, 'every Sunday evening when Sammy returned he would say he was starving because his mother had spent the money down the pub.'

'Money?'

'Yes, Sammy's mother would only have him home if she was given twenty-five pounds for food for Sammy.'

'Money to feed her own kid,' I said in disbelief.

Alan was studying me with amusement, enjoying the genuine shocked look on my face.

'Then why give her the money?'

'Because without it she wouldn't have any contact with him at all. Social services have to actively promote the up-bringing of children by their families and Sammy's mother knows this.'

If anyone else had told me I would have thought it was a joke but Alan never joked. He just pushed his sensible glasses up his nose, the thick lenses highlighting his dull grey eyes and said, 'At one point she didn't have any home contact with Sammy for six months.'

'A whole six months?' I echoed the words back. 'Why?'

'She'd rented his bedroom out to a couple of Polish immigrants.'

*

Acorn House worked on a shift schedule designed so there was always a ratio of three staff on shift to the eight children. Most times you wouldn't leave work until after eleven at night because the kids would be slow to settle. By the time I had made the journey home, it would be midnight. I would be lucky to get four hours kip before I had to be back on shift at 7.30 to try and get the kids up for school.

Chapter 4

It was decided that Charlie would stay at Acorn House on a short-term placement for three months until he could return to his adoptive parents.

It wasn't long before Charlie formed a friendship with a kid named Eddy. Eddy had lost both his mother and father in a car crash when he was twelve. After that Eddy went to live with his grandmother but he would often steal from her and each time she would forgive him.

When Eddy stole her cash card and spent three hundred pounds on drugs Eddy's grandmother told the social worker she couldn't heal the boy's wounds or cope with his behaviour any longer.

Eddy was thirteen when he entered care. He was now 16 and big for his age, six-foot-two and skinny with a nasty complexion and completely off the rails. Alcohol, cannabis, cocaine, you name it and Eddy had and would try it. It was Eddy who Charlie palled up with.

I helped Charlie move out of the emergency bedroom into one located next to the upstairs fire exit. He was still waiting for a few more of his personal items from home to be delivered by his mother, but otherwise he had all he needed. Helping him get his room right gave me the opportunity to bring up a few of the things that were worrying me. For one thing, all the kids in Acorn House smoked cigarettes and used cannabis. If a kid came in that never smoked they soon started. Smoking in care was a functional currency that all the kids traded in. If one kid had cigarettes then all the kids wanted to be their friend. I really didn't want Charlie to get drawn into the habit.

'Charlie, I notice you don't smoke. Take my advice and keep it that way.' I closed the bedroom door over in case there was anyone on the landing.

'Also don't start smoking all that other shit,' I said in a low voice. 'I tell you kid that stuff will fuck you over. You start that shit and you'll just end up a fucking dead head.' Speaking straight to kids in this way was forbidden and although the kids swore all the time at staff and each other, staff members were expected to set a good example. I could understand this and was careful never to swear in front of certain staff or certain kids but with Charlie it was okay.

Charlie shrugged his shoulders, 'No worries Jerry lad.'

'Good, now, what about your mum? When are you seeing her?'

He looked at me and shrugged and for the first time it hit me that Charlie may not want to return home.

'Oh for fuck's sake Charlie, you don't want to stay here? Don't you want to get home to your family?'

He lowered his head. 'I don't know,' he said, his voice flat.

'Don't be foolish. You'll regret it,' I said keeping it light but I could see there were things on his mind, things he needed time to think through and I didn't want to push him any further on the matter.

'What about school? You must stay in school.'

'It's a mission, Jerry, getting the train and then a bus. Eddy said I can get my social worker to move me to a nearer school.' I cringed at the mention of Eddy.

'Eddy said?'

Charlie nodded.

'Oh well then, if Eddy said it, it must be true.' I helped Charlie hold down the corner of a poster he was attempting to put on the wall.

'If there's something you're unhappy with in school or here then see your key worker, Alan, perhaps he can sort it out.'

'He's a tit.' Charlie looked at me, waiting for my response. I felt put on the spot.

'Well, I can't say can I?' Charlie looked at me and smiled as he stuck the last corner of the poster down.

'Yeah well watch yourself with Eddy that's all am saying, *he's* a tit.'

Charlie gave me a reassuring look.

'I know, Jerry lad, I know.'

*

One Tuesday, two weeks later, I arrived for a late shift and my stomach sank. Charlie was standing on the front step with Eddy, little Sammy and Bethany all wearing the uniform of care, the Lacoste tracksuit, passing round the communal cigarette.

'Hi, how's it going?' I said, shaking my head trying to show my disappointment in Charlie. Charlie's gaze never wavered, he stood tall.

'Alright Jerry lad, how's it going?'

'Fine boys,' I said adding, 'Those things will kill you, you know. How come you're not at school Charlie?'

'I couldn't be arsed, Jerry. It's a mission.'

At Charlie's reply Eddy, Bethany and little Sammy giggled in unison. There were a few empty plastic cups scattered on the front garden, I kicked at one, half-heartedly, as I approached the door.

'He wanted to stay with us and get off his head,' added Eddy.

Now I was made aware of it I could see Charlie's pupils, big as saucers they were. I felt a huge disappointment.

'Keep up the good work kids,' I said, as I brushed past them heading towards the office.

*

Handovers are a funny thing in residential care. Someone always asks, 'Do you wanner cup of tea?' You can sense, almost taste the anticipation, as those who have been on the morning shift are eager to get out as quickly as possible. They have done their time and now it's the turn of someone else to deal with the chaos. There is also a pleasant feeling generated when so many people are occupying the office at the same time. And you know for at least a half-hour the staff ratio to kids is almost equal. There is a nice camaraderie amongst staff but even so, just below the surface and slowly gathering pace is the thought, like it or not, you're going to have to get out there with the children.

On this occasion the team leader giving the handover was, Matt, a nice guy. In all the time I had known Matt he always dressed in track suit bottoms and he seemed to have an endless supply of white *named* new trainers on his feet.

With his shoulder length hair and beard he looked a little like an overweight Jesus.

'Did little Sammy do his homework?' someone asked.

'Work? He's got that bone disease,' replied Matt.

'Bone disease?' asked Shelly, concern in her voice.

'Bone bloody idle,' said Matt.

A wave of laughter went round the room. Matt always cracked a joke or made a funny observation regarding one of the kids when giving the handover but I got the feeling no one was really fooled, they all knew it was really how Matt felt.

It had been a busy day. Matt told us that Bethany had taken an epileptic fit and he had contacted NHS Direct for advice and they'd told him as long as she hadn't injured herself then there was no need to attend the hospital. Nevertheless, Matt said it might be a good idea if she was only allowed on the internet for two hours a day tops. Margaret agreed adding that she thought the specialist Bethany was under for her epilepsy had said something along the same lines.

Bethany was a simple soul. A heavyset child, she loved her food. She had greasy hair, although every day staff encouraged her to bathe. She had lots of clothes but always wore black leggings, no matter how much staff encouraged her to wear brighter colours. Bethany had been taken into care at thirteen. When I met her she was fifteen and a bed wetter.

'Be careful around Bethany because when she goes off she's a hair puller,' said Margaret. She leaned forward and touched my knee.

'So what's the score with Bethany?' I asked. I directed my gaze at Matt.

Matt let out a slow whistle. 'In a nutshell, Bethany's granddad, who'd been living with the family, sexually abused her. He's serving a four year sentence, the cunt. The mother, the cunt, denied to the police she'd known anything about the abuse.'

'What about Bethany's father? I asked.

'He left when she was three weeks old,' said Matt.

'The mother's got a new man in her life now and Bethany has a five- month- old baby sister, Emma. The new partner,' said Margaret, crunching up her face, 'dislikes Bethany and is quite open about it.'

Night times were the worst with Bethany. She stood on the landing screaming at staff to fuck off. Eventually she would settle, laughing with you as you poured her a cup of orange juice.

'Pissy arse,' the other kids called her unless they wanted a cigarette or a quick shag. Bethany always managed to have cigarettes, not that they lasted long once the other kids got a sniff. Bethany's mother would supply her saying she couldn't handle Bethany's temper tantrums and so appeased her with cigarettes if only to 'get some fucking peace.'

Matt continued flipping the pages of the log book. I was aware that if he didn't act with haste Margaret would be unstoppable once she got talking and like everyone at the end of their shift, I could see Matt wanted to go home.

Matt continued, adding that Eddy had been taken to his Connexions interview at eleven and the woman interviewing him asked what job he would like to do in the future. Eddy had told her, 'I wanner be a drug dealer and have loads of money and birds,' said Matt, imitating Eddy's voice in an over exaggerated nasal tone.

'They just can't function outside of the Acorn House bubble can they?' This came from Mavis.

'Who gives one?' said Matt. 'Charlie never went in today either. Said he was sick. Yesterday he said he couldn't be bothered, but today he's sick or stoned. He's running with Eddy, they're up to something. I've asked Alan to do a key worker session with Charlie, set up an incentive for attending school, the usual. See if we can get him through until the summer holidays at least.'

'Pinkie and the Brain,' someone said.

'Yeah, but who's got the brain?' said Matt. He closed the log book and handed it to Shelly, the team leader for the night. 'Oh, one other thing, the U-bend that was missing from the bathroom sink turned up in little Sammy's room. He said he'd been using it to wank with.'

Shelly raised her eyebrows and let out a deep sigh.

'Let the battle commence,' Matt said, stretching his hands into the air before opening the cupboard door and taking out his coat. 'Monies are bob on,' he added nodding at the petty cash tin. 'If you need anything then give me a ring,' he said with a smile. Matt always said this when finishing a shift and I admired him for it. I admired the fact that he really did seem to care about the people he worked with.

*

Mealtimes were a wonder to behold. The kids arrived like cows at milking time. The food, prepared by the cook, was brought out on a trolley for the kids to serve themselves.

'Get me a fucking drink of milk,' shouted Eddy.

'Now Eddy, stop that language and use your manners and ask properly,' said Mavis. This late in the game Mavis had become conditioned to give this kind of response. It was a reflex, like blinking.

'Get me a fucking drink *please,'* said Eddy.

Mavis would often chat to the children at teatime about the importance of having respect and empathy for each other. The kids really did seem to listen. They would watch Mavis intensely as she paused to take a sip of water before lifting a forkful of curry and chips to her mouth.

Later, that night, little Sammy slid up next to Shelly and whispered something. I watched as Shelly's face screwed up in disgust. Shelly silently beckoned us all towards the office.

'Everyone be vigilant at mealtimes. Little Sammy has just told me that Eddy and Bethany are spitting in staff's food.'

I felt sickened. I looked over at Mavis and saw the colour drop from her face. 'Dirty pigs,' said Mavis.

'Little Sammy said it's when Eddy asks for a drink.'

'I think magicians call it misdirection,' I said, trying to lighten the mood.

'I don't care what you call it. It's dirty and disgusting,' said Mavis. Then Mavis asked what we all wanted to know. 'Did he say whose food they spat in?'

'He just said it was after the kids had plated up their own food.'

'So we all got it,' I said, tightening my mouth.

'Dirty bastards,' said Mavis.

*

She was sitting in the office when I turned up for my shift. I looked through the glass to see her sitting behind the desk. A child's file rested on her knees. I had sensed her presence as soon as I walked through the door. The home seemed different. There was quietness like in a funeral parlour.

She was at least sixty. The hair heavily dyed and the makeup plastered on thicker than a circus clown. She had large hands like a man. Matt gave me a welcoming nod when I walked in but she paid me no heed.

'So how many children have you got in at the moment?' she asked.

'Seven at the moment and the emergency bed,' said Matt.

'Well you'll be getting a few referrals pretty soon I should think. Who's outside with the children?'

'Margaret.'

'Matt, where do you keep your team plan?' she asked.

Matt pointed to the wall where the team plan hung, limp as a wet sock.

Questions, questions, like a barrister firing accusations. She turned her eyes on me. 'And you are?'

'Jerry–I'm relief staff.'

'Welcome Jerry. My name is Victoria Gray, I'm the resource manager. How are you finding it?'

'Good, thank you.'

I got the feeling you had to be careful what you said around her. It felt like she was busy making mental notes on staff, gathering information. But I couldn't tell for sure, her eyes betrayed nothing, lifeless like a child's doll.

'How have the children been Matt?' asked Victoria Gray.

'Bethany threw a cup of coffee over Margaret today after she went up for the third time to ask her to go to school,' said Matt.

Mavis laughed, it was a false laugh. 'Bless her,' she said, putting on her caring voice. 'I don't know what's worrying Bethany but there must be something on her mind. I'll have a word with her later.'

I watched, stunned, as Mavis performed like a little circus dog for the ring master. It was both shameful and pitiful.

I looked at Matt and I knew what he was thinking. But he said nothing. None of us dared. Instead we nodded our heads in agreement and sipped our tea.

'Here,' said Victoria Gray, handing Matt a white paper bag, 'I've bought some lollipops for the children. Make sure they're handed out.'

***

Chapter 5

In the summer holidays staff busied themselves organising a break for the children. All I had to do was put my name down and clear it with Kate.

'And how long will you be away?' Kate asked in a serious , her face sombre.

'A week,' I said.

'I think I can manage a week without you.' She still wasn't smiling.

'Are you sure it's okay?'

'Go. Have a good time with the kids. We'll be fine, honest,' she said smiling.

A chalet holiday in Wales. Mavis and I were to go with four of the kids: little Sammy, Bethany, Charlie and Eddy. Eddy was unable to come with the other kids, as he was due up in court on the Thursday morning for stealing the home's play station and selling it for thirty pounds. He was to follow on Thursday afternoon, after court and spend the remaining time.

Mavis was to be responsible for all spending money and as the more experienced, take charge. Mavis would stay in one room with Bethany while I bunked in with the lads. Funny thing, when the list went up calling for volunteers no names went up apart from mine.

*

I left Kate half sleeping in the early light, halfway between the waking world and the dream world. I was in a dream myself, as I still couldn't believe I would be getting paid for going on holiday. I did feel a little nervous knowing that there would only be two members of staff taking care of a group of what could be difficult kids, but perhaps away from the environment of care they'd be different, better behaved.

I left the house in silence, walked down the few steps to the car park. The street was still sleeping, the sky was clear.

The kids were up when I got there all sitting around the breakfast table, cereal bowls in front of them.

'Everything okay?' I asked.

Matt gave me a smile.

'They're okay, they just didn't realise there were two seven o' clocks in the day.'

The kids just sat, blinking in the morning light like a party of moles. Charlie, though, had a big grin on his face. He was the only one who looked awake, the energy pouring out of him like brilliant sunshine.

'Alright, Jerry lad,' he said, milk and Coco Pops dripping down his chin.

I put my bag in the office while Matt went over the spending money with Mavis. He carefully divided the money up into two white envelopes, Mavis watched as it was counted. £400 for treats, eating out and such and £140 in the other envelope to be drip fed to each of the kids over four days at a fiver a day for playing the arcades and other amusements. Matt signed over the money.

The sky looked almost purple as we stepped out into the morning. There was some gentle elbowing between little Sammy and Charlie as to who was going to sit in the front of the minibus.

'Look boys, there'll be plenty of opportunity throughout the next seven days for everyone to have a go at sitting in the front,' said Mavis, her voice full of confidence.

Charlie relented and little Sammy jumped onto the front seat, immediately turning the radio on.

'Don't think I'm listening to that racket all the way there,' said Mavis testily.

I got the slight impression that Mavis was not so full of summer joy. 'Seatbelts,' I said.

Matt waved us off. The steady early morning was in full swing with cars creeping onto the road as people headed for work, the slow hum of waking life cranking up for a new day. I felt good, content, looking forward to the time away and the prospect of giving the kids a break from the daily routine of Acorn House.

All the way there the kids went off talking, rattling like a machine gun gone wild. It was a party atmosphere and it was nice to see them all getting along. After forty-five minutes we stopped for a short break at a service station while Mavis went to the toilet. The kids stood on the step smoking.

Little Sammy spat on the floor after he'd handed over what was left of his cigarette to Bethany. The sight of young children smoking drew a long stare from an elderly man dropping a coffee cup into a concrete bin holder. Mavis returned with an armful of clingfilm,-wrapped sandwiches and proceeded to hand them out with bottles of Coke, ushering the kids back onto the minibus.

*

Monday was a matter of us getting our bearings. Once we had dropped off our bags and checked out the chalets we all met in the main reception area. It was busy with people everywhere, families, groups of kids, teenagers and little ones all rushing about, parents calling after them to, 'Be careful and walk, don't run.'

We walked through to the adjoining café. Despite the ugly appearance of the food on show behind the counter, a tantalising aroma of cheap starchy flavours hit the desire button in my stomach. Charlie and little Sammy were eyeing up the young girls and whispered something to each other as a fat woman walked by eating a hot dog. Bethany remained linked to Mavis.

Later, outside, the crash whizz sounds of the arcade captured little Sammy's attention and he came running up requesting money for the arcade. Mavis deflected him.

'Tomorrow if you're good today, I think the go-cart track is that way.' She pointed towards a sign with a little racing car on it in bright red with black cartoon exhaust fumes shooting out the back.

'That'll keep them quiet for a bit, then we can go and eat. What about you lovely, do you want to go on the go-carts?' said Mavis, smiling.

Bethany shook her head.

*

On Tuesday I was up before the kids, creeping round so I could shower before they awoke. In the interests of hygiene I tried not to let my body come into contact with the shower walls. I finished up and dried myself off before leaving the bathroom.

Although the boys were in the same room as me there was a smaller alcove added to the room containing a bed. The door was without a lock so I had to leave my belongings unattended whilst I showered. Matt had warned me to keep an eye on my stuff as little Sammy could be a sticky-fingers. Popping my head round the kids' door I saw they were sleeping soundly. I lay on the bed, picked up my watch from the bedside table. It read 6:30. I closed my eyes and drifted off.

I awoke to a trickle of soft laughter outside the cushion of sleep. It took me a moment to fully awake. I stretched out while still lying down and my shoulders clicked. I checked my watch, it was 8:15. I silently opened the boy's door. Charlie and little Sammy were standing by the window. Charlie was smoking a cigarette, blowing smoke out the open window. Little Sammy was waiting patiently, his arms wrapped around his torso and he was hopping from one foot to the other like he needed the toilet.

'Morning boys.'

For a moment I could see they were startled at being caught out but it was brief.

'Morning, Jerry lad,' Charlie grinned.

'Morning, Jerry lad,' said little Sammy following Charlie's lead.

I looked up at the smoke detector and saw it was covered by a sock tied on with a black lace. I figured what the hell, we're on holiday and they were going to do it anyway so I wouldn't come down too hard on them.

'First and last time boys, take that down and get dressed. They only serve breakfast till ten.'

After breakfast Charlie and little Sammy headed off to the go-carts with instructions to meet for dinner. They were given their five pounds for the day with strict orders not to ask adults to buy cigarettes. Bethany insisted on staying with Mavis, linking her tightly. We strolled up to the arcade, it was full of kids. Bethany brightened up when she spotted two teenage boys standing outside smoking. She ambled over to them. Mavis and I exchanged puzzled looks.

The teenage lads were eyeing up the talent as girls in little groups walked past the arcade peeking from behind their candyflosses, before turning back and giggling. One of the lads shouted something but it was inaudible against the backdrop of one-armed bandits and a cacophony of noise. The lads spotted Bethany and for a moment seemed unsure of themselves. Bethany said something and one of the lads handed her his cigarette. Bethany took a drag on it, swiftly, three times and handed it back but the lad declined with a wave of his hand. Bethany sent him her best smile and moved over by the side of the glass doors and puffed away.

That night I briefly checked in on Kate and Millie. I used the phone in the reception area. I'd not brought my mobile. Matt's warning about 'sticky fingered' Sammy making me err on the side of caution. I told Kate about the sock over the smoke alarm. She laughed and said, 'Kids eh?'

*

Wednesday was a great day. Even the people seemed happier, smiling and saying they were sorry if you accidentally bumped into them. The girl on the ice-cream stall didn't mind when I handed her a twenty-pound note and she was short of change. Little Sammy held the door open for a woman with a pushchair. Later we all had a pub lunch, Charlie, making eyes at the young girl behind the bar, eager to go up and ask for the tomato sauce.

'I'll get it,' he said, after Bethany requested it for her chips.

Everything in motion but I kept seeing important little snapshots like a subliminal message edited into a film. Snapshots of fun: go-kart racing, Charlie and little Sammy working together sending signals to each other, cutting me up on the track until little Sammy turned and sided with me and we both cut Charlie off. Snapshot: Mavis and Bethany on the sidelines giggling. Helium balloons, Charlie sucking the air out so he sounded like a high-pitched mouse, Mavis surrendering and inhaling the helium, laughter, laughter, laughter. Snapshot: waltzers, me in the middle, squashed between Charlie and little Sammy, as the man spun us like a play top. My arms stretched out, squeezing the boys tight, gravity pinning us back, our laughter the only thing able to move.

We had a lazy morning on Thursday waiting for Alan to drop off Eddy. Efficient as ever, the first thing Alan did was hand Mavis a small bottle of antibiotics, explaining Eddy was on two a day for his acne and had already taken his morning dose.

'And don't forget, even though he's on holiday he must still sign for his medication,' said Alan.

'How did it go at court?' I said.

'He got a three-month extension on his previous supervision order,' said Alan.

'Wankers,' laughed Eddy, throwing his bag onto the floor.

'Cut it out,' said Alan sternly.

Alan didn't stay long. He took a brief look around the rooms, pushing his glasses up, as he inspected the bedrooms.

'Have they not made their beds yet?' asked Alan.

Mavis pretended not to hear him and instead turned to Bethany.

'Come on Bethany, get dressed love, you're on holiday. Let's go and enjoy ourselves.'

If Alan understood what Mavis was getting at it didn't show on his face.

'Have you got time for a cuppa before you head back?' I asked.

'No, no, I have to get back to Acorn House. I'm doing a full day.'

Mavis hustled Bethany into the bedroom.

Alan was gone by two. Eddy quickly got the measure of the place asking for his five-pound daily allowance and then off he went with Charlie and little Sammy.

Friday:

'For fuck's sake,' said little Sammy. He was standing on a chair leaning out of the window, his body as far out as he could get without falling. Eddy and Charlie laughing only served to heighten his anger. 'For fuck's sake, yer knob,' he shouted.

'What's going on?' I said.

'That wanker,' said little Sammy, pointing at Eddy, 'he's thrown me trainer out the window.'

'You're the wanker, lad,' said Eddy, laughing.

I walked over to the window.

'Okay, let me look,' I said, guiding little Sammy down from the chair.

The trainer had landed in a freshly made flower bed. A light drizzle had started to fall and the material of the trainer was getting darker, as the water soaked through the shoe.

'Go and get his trainer,' I said, without looking at Eddy.

'It wasn't me.'

'Eddy, stop fooling about and go and get his trainer.'

'Fuck that,' said Eddy.

I pulled the window shut and walked back towards my sleeping area.

'Okay, suit yourself, I said. 'There goes your five quid for today.'

'Fuck off, I didn't do nothing. Yer little twat,' said Eddy, slapping little Sammy across the head.

'Hey, cut it out,' I said. 'Any more messing about and we'll go home.'

That seemed to calm the moment but it was short-lived.

'See what you've done now yer little fucker,' said Eddy, pushing little Sammy in the chest.

'Right, that's it,' I shouted.

I put myself between Eddy and little Sammy. Eddy's stare met mine. He licked his lips and grinned, sniffed and stuck his chin out, rising himself up as tall as he could.

'Yeah, that's right, side with that little shit.'

I could hear my heart pounding in my ears, sending me the message to calm down and quick. The way Eddy spoke to me made me feel degraded. I didn't like it.

'Look,' I said calmly, 'I just want us all to have a nice holiday. Go and get his trainer then we can go out and everyone gets their five quid.'

It was a crucial moment and the balance of power could have gone either way.

'I'll go,' said Charlie, walking out the door. He returned a minute later with the trainer, handing it to little Sammy. Little Sammy brushed the soil off with his hand, banging the trainer against the wall to remove the more stubborn bits.

'Hey, yer mucky pup,' I said, 'you're putting it all over the carpet.'

'Sorry.'

'It's okay. Now, let's go and enjoy ourselves.'

The weather had changed. Even the neon lights of the arcades seemed less vibrant. Mothers had the protective plastics drawn over pushchairs, trying to steer the buggies with one hand whilst holding umbrellas with the other. Most had a second child gripping onto the pushchair, holding their faces up to the rain.

We all met at the pub for lunch. Mavis and Bethany were at the bar placing their order while I went over the menu for the hundredth time. Charlie came running in, laughing and out of breath. Mavis shot me an *Is everything okay glance.*

'What's up?' I asked.

'Nothing, just starving that's all.'

'What's so funny?'

Charlie flopped down in the seat opposite me and picked up a menu.

'Little Sammy just bought Eddy a can of Coke and when Eddy opened it, it all exploded over his new tracky. Fucking Coke everywhere,' he laughed.

There was a young couple with a child at the next table and they looked over at us.

'Charlie,' I said, nodding towards the table.

'Oh, sorry.' He continued in a lower voice, 'There was Coke everywhere. Little Sammy must have shook the can before he gave it to him.'

Mavis came over carrying a tray of soft drinks.

'Decided what you're having yet, Jerry?'

'Yeah, scampi and chips.'

'That'll make a change,' she said. 'What about you Charlie?'

'Still looking.'

'Where's the other two?' said Mavis.

'They'll be here in a mo,' said Charlie, 'they're just cleaning up.'

Mavis shot me a puzzled look.

'I'll explain later,' I said. 'It's nothing serious.'

Mavis returned to the bar. I waited until Charlie had taken a sip of his drink.

'So how come little Sammy paid for Eddy's can of Coke?'

Charlie wiped his mouth with the back of his hand before he spoke.

'He'd spent his on bifftas.'

'How did he get served?'

'Got someone to go in for him.'

He took another drink, this time a long gulp, emptying more than half the glass.

'Thanks for today, Charlie.'

'What?'

'You know, calming it with Eddy, getting little Sammy's trainer.'

'No probs, Jerry, lad.'

The door to the pub slammed open causing everyone in the room to look round. Little Sammy and Eddy burst in like a stag party, arms around each other, laughing.

'Alright, boys, settle down,' I said.

Eddy snatched up the menu.' What's to eat? I'm fuckin' starving.'

'Eddy, watch your language, there's young children in here,' I said.

'Yeah, whatever.'

Little Sammy started rubbing his fingers through his short hair.

'What's wrong with your hair?' I asked, rubbing my hand over his head, 'It's all sticky.'

'Eddy poured Coke on it.'

Mavis came over. 'What would you like to drink Eddy?'

'Whisky,' said Eddy, half-smiling.

'In your dreams. What about you, Sammy, Coke?'

'He's had enough Coke for today,' said Eddy, laughing.

We all laughed except Mavis who wasn't in on the joke.

Lunch time went off without a hitch, the trouble with Eddy from earlier in the day forgotten.

'Right I'm off for a biffta,' said Eddy, standing up and pushing his chair back.

'Bagsy seconds,' said Charlie.

'Bagsy thirds,' said little Sammy.

'Can I come?' said Bethany.

'Suppose so, pissy arse,' said Eddy.

'Eddy, cut it out will you?' I said.

We sat there enjoying the moment's peace, Mavis taking the time to go through a few receipts.

'You know she hasn't wet the bed once since we've been here,' said Mavis.

'Good, must be the fresh air.'

Mavis laughed. 'What fresh air?' She clicked her purse shut. 'Where did Eddy get the cigarettes?'

'Charlie said he got someone to go in for him.'

'Yeah, they always find a way. At least they don't seem to have brought any pot with them,' she said, adding, 'I just don't trust that Eddy, he's a mean one.'

In a strange way it felt good to hear Mavis say that about Eddy.

*

We returned late to our chalet. I dropped into bed exhausted. The boys settled quickly, little Sammy even following instructions to shower and get the Coke out of his hair before bed. Sleep quickly came.

The banging penetrated my sleep. I moved sluggishly out of my slumber searching in the dark for my pants while feeling along the wall for the light switch. Still the banging persisted at the door. I flicked the switch, my eyes momentarily retracting from the light. I checked my watch. It was 3:35 in the morning. My first thought was it must be Mavis, an emergency. Perhaps there had been an accident.

Standing in front of me was a man; pot-bellied and vested in boxer shorts and bare feet, a squat little Juggernaut of a man with tattoos running down his large arms.

'Where's the little fucks?' he shouted.

At first the question didn't register and then it hit me. None of the boys had come out to see what all the noise was about.

'I'm sorry mate, what's the problem?'

'What's the fucking problem?' I'll tell yer what the fucking problem is. Your fucking lad and two of his mates have just been in my chalet.'

By now some of the lights from the other chalets had come on and a few faces leaned out of windows to see what all the commotion was.

'Okay mate, calm down and I'll have a word with them. Was anything taken?'

'No. I'm sure it would have been but I heard the little cunts smashing around, but the fuckers got out the window before I could get me hands on them. The three of them came in here,' he said, pointing towards the window, which was wide open.

I opened the boys' door and flicked the light. All three were sound asleep.

'Okay, lads, get up.'

'What's happening?' said Charlie.

'Look, stop with the fooling and get up. There's a big fella at the door, wants to see you all and he's pretty pissed.'

All three of them exchanged looks.

'I wondered where all the banging was coming from,' said little Sammy, pushing his bed clothes off.

'Always sleep in your clothes do you?' I said.

He didn't answer but the game was up. They all sat up revealing they were dressed.

'When you're ready boys, outside.'

I thought about sending Charlie to wake Mavis but then thought it best to wait to see how things panned out. I didn't want Bethany adding to the problem.

The three of them huddled behind me, serious looks on their faces. The man's face tightened, he went to speak and I held up my hand to stop him.

'This man says you boys were just in his chalet.'

'What?' Eddy replied.

I looked at little Sammy, he bent his head low and shook it slowly in denial.

'Charlie?' I said.

Charlie looked up and tentatively gave a nod.

'Charlie, are you telling me what this gentleman says is true?'

'Yes,' he whispered, 'it was just for a laugh, that's all.'

'I told you it was them. The little fuckers,' said the man.

'Fuck yerself, yer fat cunt.'

'Cut it out Eddy,' I snapped.

The man moved forward and I placed myself in his way.

'Look, mate, you can't come in here.'

'Are you going to let him speak to me that way?'

The man's fists were clenched and his arms tensed, the veins sticking out, his eyes zeroed in on mine.

'Look, if we all just calm down,' I said, trying to stall for time, desperately searching my mind for a better idea.

'Boys, go back in your room, please.'

They shuffled off, Eddy grinning. I turned to the man.

'You said nothing was taken, right?'

'Yeah, but that's not the point.'

'Look, mate, I work for Social Services. These kids are in care. My advice to you is to phone the police and let them deal with it. There's very little I can do. I'm just their carer while they're on holiday.'

His face relaxed, the veins in his arms faded.

'Orphans?'

'Yeah, mate, orphans.'

Fuck it I thought, might as well go all the way and get the full sympathy vote. 'They've got a few issues, if you know what I mean? Obviously, I will sanction them but it'll have very little impact. You might want to consider calling the police.'

I could see him start to waver, soften, so I pushed on.

'It's really in your hands, mate.'

The man lifted the bottom of his vest and used it to wipe his nose.

'Let it go,' he said.

He tapped a finger to the side of his head, 'They've got problems?'

I nodded.

'But if it happens again I go to the police.'

'Absolutely,' I said, 'absolutely.'

Mavis, after learning what went on decided to go home a day early. I argued it was unfair on Bethany who hadn't been involved.

'They all knew the ground rules before we left,' said Mavis.

Throughout the drive back to Acorn House, Eddy sat in the front switching radio stations every two seconds, the music so loud my head ached.

It was after the holiday I was offered a permanent contract.

***

Chapter 6

I was on a late shift with Matt and a care worker named Mary. It was a quiet evening. Tea time passed in an unusually pleasant manner and afterwards most of the kids occupied themselves by watching television. I read the newspaper, catching up on world events when Matt motioned me over to the bottom of the stairs.

'Listen,' he said tilting his head. 'I think the lads are up to something.' I listened but could hear nothing except the pounding bass of a rap song coming from one of the bedrooms. I now knew enough to know that whenever it was this calm something was going on. Most probably there was cannabis in the building and someone was skinning up.

All the kids knew pot was not allowed on the premises, but it was difficult to police. We made our way up the stairs as quietly as we could whilst Mary stayed downstairs to keep an eye on the kids watching telly.

The upper floors of Acorn House were like a rabbit warren leading off in three directions. Here there were three bedrooms all with the doors left open apart from the one directly in front of us. I nodded to Matt.

'This one.' From behind the closed door of Charlie's bedroom there was the boom of music and underneath the light laughter of two voices. Matt got his key ready and knocked on the door.

'Who's that?'

It was Charlie.

'We're coming in,' Matt said.

'Wait a minute will yer?' Charlie replied.

'Who's in there with you?' asked Matt.

'No one, I'm not dressed that's all and you can't just come in.'

This was a new one on me. I had never heard Charlie get all *I know my rights* shit before.

'We're coming in,' said Matt putting his key in the door.

Charlie was lying on his bed. The single window open, but this did nothing to disguise the smell of cigarette smoke mixed with the aroma of pot. I looked around to see where the second voice had come from. A poster of the rap artist Tupac stared down at me from the wall, next to him was a cannabis leaf drawn in black ink with the words, *respect the weed* written underneath. I stepped over the dirty clothing and CD cases that littered the plain carpeted floor and turned down the volume on Charlie's boom box.

'Did you do that?' I asked pointing to the artwork on the wall.

'Yeah, it's good init?'

'Respect the weed,' I read out loud. 'I think you should respect yourself,' I said.

'Where's Eddy?' Matt asked turning to the matter in hand. 'You know the rules. You're not allowed in each other's rooms with the door shut.'

'Yeah, but that's a crap rule.'

'Look, we've been over this, it's there to protect you. How many times does stuff go missing out of the rooms in here? You're right. It shouldn't be that way, but unfortunately some kids steal off each other and sometimes bully each other. Now come on Charlie, where's Eddy?' said Matt.

'I don't know. He's not here.'

'Charlie, have you been smoking in here?' I asked.

'No,' he said, grinning at me.

I bent down to look under Charlie's bed – all clear. I turned my attention to the wardrobe. Eddy was there giggling, attempting to hide his lanky body behind a solitary shirt.

'Oh yer bastard,' he said, stepping out of the wardrobe. As I've said there was something that unsettled me about Eddy. When you looked into his eyes there was nothing there, no contact, they were dead. I never felt entirely safe or at ease when dealing with him. There had been a few times when I thought he was testing me, pushing me, trying to get a reaction.

'Alright lads, you've had yer fun, out of the room now please,' Matt said.

'Nah, I can't be arsed,' said Eddy, sitting down on the floor after he'd kicked away some clothing that was lying there.

'Come on Eddy.' I looked at Charlie and nodded, hoping for some support from him, for him to lead by example, but he stayed silent.

'Fuck you, Knob Head,' Eddy spat the words out laughing. I hated that, I hated when one of them spoke to you with no respect whatsoever. I had no answer. I waited for Matt to take control. He was the senior, he had experience and he would know what to do next.

'Charlie,' Matt said, 'if you come out then so will he.'

'Don't go Charlie lad, stay here. Let's have some tunes and get stoned,' said Eddy, turning the volume back up on the boom box. I looked at Charlie, pleading with him to do the right thing. I could tell the situation made him uncomfortable, but I could also tell he didn't want to lose face in front of Eddy. At that moment Mary's voice came up the stairs, 'Everything all right up there?'

'Yeah no probs!' I shouted back. I turned back to look at Charlie and was about to speak when Eddy screamed at the top of his voice down to Mary, 'Fuck off yer donkey; no one likes yer, fat arse!'

'Hey what are you talking to people like that for?' I said, unable to hide the disdain in my voice. 'Look Eddy,' I breathed, calming my voice. 'We've all had a laugh, now let's start again. We can have a joke and a laugh, but you can't be in each other's bedrooms with the door shut, you know that. And you can't be smoking bifftas or anything else in the home, it's against health and safety, plus if any of you have got pot we'll have to call the police. This is a children's home.'

Eddy's tone changed. He grew calm and his face relaxed.

'I was only having a laugh with yer.' He paused. 'If we come down stairs can we have some money to go the shop to get a magazine for an activity?'

'We'll talk about it downstairs,' Matt said, unwilling to commit himself to anything concrete. This, I was to learn, was always a good method of working. Never make promises, and it seemed to be having an effect. Eddy was up and off the floor, Charlie following Eddy's lead and getting up off the bed.

'Good lads, you know it makes sense,' Matt said, doing his best Del Trotter impersonation, making Eddy and Charlie laugh. This is more like it, I thought but suddenly without any warning Eddy's rhythm changed.

'Nah, I can't be arsed,' he said, sitting himself back down on the floor. 'I know what you'll do. Once we go downstairs you won't give us any money.'

'Okay,' I said looking at Matt, neither of us sure if the joke was still on or not. This was getting tedious. 'If you're not gonna get out then I'll put you out.'

'Go on then,' said Eddy laughing.

I knew deep inside as soon as I said it, it was a mistake but instead of listening to that inner voice I took hold of Eddy's left foot and began pulling him along the floor towards the door, Matt played along taking hold of the other foot. Eddy continued to laugh.

'Ah you're out lad,' laughed Charlie.

Eddy tried to slow his exit by making a grab for the leg of the bed but missed and was edged nearer the door inch by inch. Perhaps it was Charlie laughing, I don't know but as I watched Eddy his face became distorted, twisted, his teeth drawn back. He squirmed on the floor like a large fish being landed, impossible to contain.

'Fuck off!' he screamed. Matt must have sensed the change right away and let go, but I kept hold a moment longer than intended. Eddy was up and at me. I stepped back, a kick narrowly missing my jaw. I was not going to take this.

'Come on then hard man. Let's have it,' I roared. It was a guttural cry. It flowed through me like a sharp pain. Eddy drew back and spat in my face. The action froze me, the spit thick and vile slid down my face invading my mouth, invading me. I could smell him on me. In that moment I wanted to drop him, rip out his eyes, punch him till he bled. Instead I stood there, fists clenched, the anger spilling out of me in great sobs of rage. I turned, overcome and punched a hole in the wall, 'BASTARD!' I shouted. 'BASTARD!'

*

Downstairs in the office I was shaking, angry with myself, frightened I would be finished up. Matt told me to stay in the office until I was calm,

'Matt, what about the hole in the wall? I'm fucked.'

‘That hole was there before,’ Matt said with a wink, as he left the office. My mind went through the episode: how could I justify this? How did it get out of control so fast? Surely Eddy would make a complaint; of that I was sure and the children’s complaints officer would certainly have a case. Okay I lost my temper, but I didn’t hit the kid. God, a kid, how did that sound? The little bastard went for me, the dirty little cunt spat on me. That must count for something.

I don’t know exactly how long I sat there contemplating my future, running through my defence. A light knocking on the office door broke my thoughts. It had to be a kid, as all staff had keys. I got up and crossed to the door. Through the glass I could see Charlie’s face. He nodded for me to open the door.

‘You alright Jerry lad?’

‘Yeah,’ I said, doing my best to look calm. ‘How’s the wall?’

‘No probs, you can’t see it. I’ve put Tupac over it.’ He looked at me smiling, ‘and I’ve sorted it with Eddy, he was just being a tit.’

There and then I made a promise to myself not to lose control again, no matter how much I was pushed. It wasn't worth it.

*

That night I crept into the bedroom, slowly undressing in the dark, knowing by memory where every piece of furniture was situated. I slumped onto the edge of the bed not wanting to disturb Kate but selfishly wanting her to wake so I could talk. I guess it was about here the thought of having Charlie come and stay with us first occurred to me.

I pulled back the covers and dropped into bed. I let out a long desperate sigh. I closed my eyes knowing that tonight sleep would be difficult or might not come at all. 'Kate.' I whispered. 'Kate, are you asleep?'

She moved. 'I was,' she said sleepily. 'What's up?'

'Nothing,' I answered, now feeling guilty for disturbing her.

'You didn't wake me for nothing.'

I told her everything.

'It's just that if Charlie stays there much longer,' I said, sitting up on my elbows, 'he's just going to end up like Eddy.'

'Jerry, you can only do your best.'

'It doesn't matter how much I try Kate. While he's in there any effort on my part is a drop in the ocean.'

Kate's hand lay on my chest, the rhythm of my heart amplified by the connection. For a moment the sweet smell of her perfume filled my nostrils but I could still smell the stench of Eddy's breath and I sat up on the edge of the bed.

'What's up?'

'Nothing, I'm going to shower. I feel dirty after that bastard spitting on me. Besides, I'm not going to sleep tonight, I'm too wound up.'

I stood up and stretched out, the tension clicking in my joints. My neck was wound like a spring.

'Why don't you take the day off tomorrow? Phone in sick.'

'I can't.'

The shower felt good.

That weekend Kate and I took a trip to Blackpool, Millie holding our hands, swinging between us as we strolled down the prom.

It felt good relaxing on the beach. I made a sand mermaid with Millie, who was excited, filling her bucket, helping Daddy pat down the sand and flattening it into shape.

I watched with Kate, as Millie collected shells, putting them in her bucket, as if they were precious gems.

'She's having fun,' I said.

'She certainly is,' said Kate, dipping into her picnic bag and offering me a piece of chicken.

'Millie, don't you go too near that water,' Kate shouted.

A man walked by leading a group of donkeys, children riding on their backs, their laughter coming in spurts. The donkeys looked worn and tired.

'I've always thought that cruel,' said Kate.

'What's that?'

'Those poor donkeys, the way they're paraded up and down all day.'

The man shouted something at the donkeys, inaudible against the backdrop of the sea and children playing.

'There are worse things in the world, babe.'

Kate handed me a small bottle of beer and sat closer, positioning herself so she could still see Millie.

'You mean like your kids at work?' she said.

I watched as Millie lined up her shells, carefully placing them side by side.

'Yeah, like the kids in care.'

A slight breeze had turned up the corner of the towel we were sitting on.

Kate patted it back down before bringing her knees up to her chest.

'It's really shaken you up, that episode with Eddy, hasn't it?'

In truth I'd not planned to talk about work but being with Kate, watching, Millie so carefree and full of joy did make me think about Charlie's future.

'It's funny, Kate, but up until now I've turned up for work believing I can make a difference but never giving much thought about what happens to these kids when they leave care. I just know it won't be good for Charlie. The longer he's there the more contaminated he'll become.'

A beach ball bounced in to us. I looked up and a man and two small boys all said, 'Sorry.' I laughed and threw the ball back. I heard the man tell the boys to be careful as they moved a little further up the beach.

'Contaminated, you said.'

'Yeah, contaminated, the longer Charlie's there the worse he'll get, until he's just another Eddy. Charlie's a good kid, but he won't be for long. He protected me, Kate. He put that poster over the hole because he knew Eddy was wrong. That means there's hope.'

Kate's hand touched mine.

'Maybe you should think about protecting him.'

'How?' I said.

She looked me in the eyes, her gaze intense and serious.

'Bring him to live with us.'

'To live with us?' I said.

'All I'm saying is, I wouldn't mind. If that's what you want.'

Millie came running over with her bucket of shells.

'Look, Mummy, you could make a necklace.'

'Oh, they're beautiful, Millie, thank you,' said Kate, brushing the sand from Millie's knees and hugging her.

The clanging of bells drifted into earshot, as the donkeys paraded back up the beach. Then came the musical bells from an ice cream van, its arrival causing a stampede of small children.

That night I couldn't sleep, thinking about what Kate had said. I knew if Charlie stayed much longer in care that he was going to change. Smoking pot and not going to school were just the early symptoms. But if I took him in it was a massive commitment and what about the impact on Millie? She was, and had to be, my main priority. Perhaps I was being over-cautious; bringing Charlie into our family might turn out to be the best thing I ever did.

I took a late night stroll along the prom and watched the tide. The sounds of late night revellers filtered in and out. I breathed deeply, the air crisp. The sandcastles the children had built earlier had been swept away by the relentless sea, nothing diverting nature from its path, the sand helpless against its power.

***

Chapter 7

A meeting was arranged by Charlie's social worker to tackle the problem regarding his education. Charlie's key-worker Alan would be there but Charlie asked if I could also attend. Carol, the home's manager, said if it helped Charlie it would be okay and that it was important Charlie had an advocate to help him express his wishes and feelings. *Wishes and feelings* was a phrase alongside *short-term placement* I would later come to loathe.

Alongside Charlie there were a number of professionals: the educational social worker for looked-after children, the learning mentor from Charlie's school, the educational welfare officer, the designated teacher, Carol, and the head of the school, a Mrs. Macintyre. Charlie's mother and father declined to attend. The Chair, a thin middle-aged bearded man whose dull grey suit looked like it had seen better days, began the meeting by telling us why we were there. Then after each of us had introduced ourselves and after a tray of tea, coffee and biscuits was served, the meeting began.

'So, Charlie what's the problem with school?' asked the Chair.

'I just don't want to go any more. I don't see the point.'

'What has Charlie's attendance been like of late?' asked the Chair of nobody in particular.

Sheets of paper were quickly handed round by the social worker.

'As I'm sure Mrs. Macintyre will know Charlie's attend–'

'Excuse me are there any more copies?'

This came from the educational welfare officer, a red-faced lady with bobbed black hair and a lot of mascara.

'So sorry. I must not have done enough, would people mind sharing?" asked the social worker.

The noise of shuffling papers went around the room.

The social worker gathered herself and continued.

'When Charlie first came into Acorn House his attendance was a hundred percent. His grades were above average and he was and remains a popular pupil at his school and very well liked by his teachers.'

Mrs. Macintyre nodded in agreement and there were smiles all round.

'So, Charlie, what's the problem?' repeated the Chair, his voice warm and understanding.

'I don't like school.'

'Charlie, education is important. How are you going to get a job when you leave school? How are you going to earn a living?'

Charlie shrugged his shoulders and stared at the floor.

'If I came and picked you up every day and we worked together to catch up on the work that you've missed, would you come back?' asked the learning mentor, a shaven-headed man in a suit.

Silence.

Mrs. Macintyre shifted uncomfortably in her chair crossing her legs and dropping her paper onto the floor. As she bent to pick it up I caught Charlie's eye as he focused on the window behind her. I followed his gaze. The clouds were grey and broken across the dull sky. On the ground there was a flock of seagulls walking as one body across an open field, mimicking the falling rain with their feet, trying to get the worms to come to the surface. Eddy's face suddenly appeared pressed against the window like a sucker fish. He drew back blowing smoke rings into the air, Bethany behind him grinning, laughing at Eddy's party trick, waiting for her turn on the communal cigarette.

'Can someone draw the blinds please?' I said, pointing at the window.

Charlie was up immediately, as if his chair had caught fire and out the door.

'Eddy,' he shouted. 'Save me on that biffta!'

'Charlie,' I pleaded. 'Come back, this is important.'

The professionals exchanged looks before their eyes came to rest on me. I felt I should say something.

'Would you like me to go and see if I can get him to return?' I directed my question to the room. I could see the kids through the window huddled together laughing. Their breath caught in the cold air, Charlie waiting for his turn on the cigarette, Bethany edging her way in, waiting for the scraps.

'Perhaps we can continue without him for the time being. I'm sure he will rejoin us when he's had his cigarette,' said the Chair, checking his watch, helping himself to another chocolate biscuit.

After ten minutes or so Charlie rejoined the meeting. As he sank down into the chair next to me he said, 'I can't go to school, I've got no good shoes.'

The Chair, seizing the opportunity, brushed the crumbs from the corner of his mouth and asked the manager if this was true. For a moment Carol looked flustered, but she quickly regained her composure.

Carol was a small woman. She dressed conservatively and her shoulder-length hair had strands of grey in its black waves. She was well-educated and had been in the job a long time and had taken the opportunities her career presented. I respected her because she always treated people with respect and because others told me how she worked her way up from the bottom and knew every aspect of the job.

'Of course Charlie's got shoes, but if he hasn't we, of course, would provide him with uniform, shoes, transport, that is if it got him to return to his education. You have a full uniform don't you Charlie?'

Charlie stopped fidgeting with his chair where he'd managed to pull out some of the stitch work from one corner.

'My jumper's got holes in it.' He turned his attention back to the corner of his chair. So it was as simple as shoes then I thought. Of course it was not *that* simple. Charlie wanted a certain type of shoes, Rock Port, £200.00 a shot–the in thing.

'It could work as part of your incentive plan. Your key worker,' she nodded at Alan, 'could draw up a contract. Let's say if you attend education for a week and your behaviour is acceptable say…' Carol motioned with her hand towards the headmistress.

Mrs. Macintyre nodded back, an affirmative smile.

'For one week, then we can look at buying Charlie some of these… Rock Port shoes. Until then are you okay to use the shoes you have?' asked Carol.

'Yeah, laughin'. No probs,' said Charlie, happier than I'd seen him in a long time. He gave me a wink. I looked to Alan but if he was on to it he kept quiet. I couldn't believe that they were all falling for it.

*

Charlie returned to school looking smart in his uniform and the following week, as agreed, got his £200 Rock Port shoes. The week after Charlie told staff his new shoes had been stolen out of his bedroom. They were never found, but word filtered through to staff from little Sammy that Charlie had sold them for £30.

Charlie and Eddy were missing from care that weekend. They returned late Sunday. I asked Charlie where he'd been.

'Getting stoned,' he said with a big smile. 'Getting stoned.'

*

I confided in Matt I was worried about Charlie.

'Look,' Matt said, 'they're all the same. Once they come in here none of them ever go to school. Trying to find a kid that goes to school in care is like trying to find rocking horse shit. There's nothing you can do. And it's no good feeling bad about it. Social Services couldn't give a fuck. As long as they've offered them '*choices*' and put things in place, had a meeting to record it, no one cares. It's just arse covering. We're just baby sitters.'

Matt screwed up a piece of paper he'd been doodling on and threw it basketball like into the bin.

'Think about it. The Children's Act states they must always put the welfare of the child at the centre of everything, particularly education.' He flopped back in his chair and put his feet up on the desk. 'So they place the kid in a home, miles away from his school. How long do you think he's gonna get up at the crack of dawn, to catch the train to school? I'll tell yer, not long. Jerry, make no mistake, even if his school was round the corner he still won't go, not while he's in here. Not while he can sit off with all these wasters.'

Matt moved his feet off the desk and leaned over. When he spoke it was almost a whisper.

'It's got fuck all to do with the welfare of the child. It's to do with money and it would cost too much to put Charlie in a placement closer to here or send him to residential school. This,' he said, tapping the desk with his finger, 'is the cheapest option.'

Over the last few weeks I had read fervently Bowlby's Theory of Attachment.

I read Erikson and his theory of psychosocial development. Then there were others: Rutter, Beckett and Freud. The theories and constructs, like the authors, went on and on: 'All behaviour is communication.' It sure didn't feel like that when a kid spat in your face.

I read up on procedures, none of which helped Charlie. *He* simply *chose* to opt out of school. Matt was right. The whole system was shot; a system that advocated choice and then complained when the kids made the wrong choices.

'So what happens now?' I asked. 'Charlie is only on a short-term placement until they can get him back home.'

Matt shook his head and laughed, 'Jerry, Jerry, my son you've a lot to learn. There is no such thing as a short-term placement. Once in here the social workers forget about them. The parents forget about them. It's like Centre Parcs in here. Never Never Land. Activities every night, bowling, snooker, a hundred and fifty pounds clothing money every six weeks. The cinema and money on tap, come and go as you like, talk to adults any way you want and no consequences. If you were a kid, would you leave? Would you want to go home? How the fuck can any parents compete with that? I work and I can't.'

I thought about this for a moment. 'I guess not,' I said with a sigh.

'There are no child protection issues with Charlie. He's not been beaten or sexually abused. He's only a section 20 they could have just put a family suppor–'

'A section 20?' Matt's look told me how new I still was to the game.

'You have section 20s and section 31s. A section 31 is a Full Care Order. Parental consent is shared with Social Services. Charlie is a section 20, which means he's only here on a voluntary basis.'

'Voluntary?' I said in disbelief.

'Voluntary. His parents still have full parental consent. They can take him home anytime they want. Of course he's got to *want* to go back, but I don't think he does. He's happy here. The bottom line is even if his parents said he's going home tomorrow we can't make him and neither can they.' He paused. 'Even if Charlie did want to go home I don't think they want him now anyway, what with his pot smoking and not going to school. They'll just say they can't handle him and refuse.'

'Wouldn't they be done for abandonment?'

'Not at fifteen. No way would the authority go down that path. Now, if he was a dog…' said Matt laughing. 'I laugh Jerry, but I'll tell you what is funny,' he stopped for moment, took a handkerchief that had seen better days out of his pocket, and blew his nose before continuing, 'even though their kids are in here, kept by the tax payer, the parents still claim the family allowance even though they shouldn't and nothing gets done. Now, sometimes when the social workers do a Fin One they can—'

'What's a fin one?'

Matt placed his feet back upon the desk and let out a slow yawn stretching his arms and fingers out, his chair creaking under the effort.

'A financial assessment. If the parents work, like Charlie's mum and dad, they're supposed to contribute, financially,' Matt waved his hand indicating the home, 'to his up keep here, but most of the kids, their parents don't work and even when they do most social workers don't do Fin Ones, as they say if the parents are made to pay and can't or won't, which is more like it, it may force a vulnerable child back into a home where they don't belong, depriving parents and the child of the service. And I guess there is a little truth in that, but that's why they're supposed to do a fin one. If the assessment says they can't afford it, then they can't afford it and they would get it for free. *Jesus* my own mother had to sell her home to pay for her care and no one gave a fuck how vulnerable she was. No pay no care. And she'd worked all her life.'

I sank into my chair. 'So you don't think Charlie will go home?' I said, chewing at the end of my biro.

'Charlie won't go home, and once he's sixteen they will bin him off in the cheapest way possible: B&B, hostel, whatever. You see, at sixteen everything changes for section 20s. If they're not keeping to their care plan, going to school or some other excuse for an education, Social Services can legally discharge them. The only difference is by then he'll be fucked, criminal record, no education and a smackhead. It's what they call a self-fulfilling prophecy.' He shrugged. 'What can yer do?'

'What if I took him to live with me? You know, see if we can foster him. What would his chances be?'

If Matt was surprised by what I'd said it never showed, almost as if he'd been expecting it.

'What does your missus say?'

'She fine with it. It was her idea after I told her about him.'

Matt pulled at the end of his beard. 'She's fine with it because she doesn't see the full picture.'

'Others must have taken kids home in the past,' I challenged.

Matt nodded. 'They have but nine times out of ten the results have been a disaster. You have a kid of your own, what if she becomes infected by Charlie? Pull a face if you want but I've seen it happen, mate.'

'Oh come on, Charlie's not carrying some incurable disease.'

'Okay, so what about when he starts robbing off you?'

I felt like Matt was just creating problems where there weren't any.

'He's not a robber now,' I said.

Matt laughed. 'How do you think him and Eddy have always got bifftas or pot? What did he do with his school shoes?' Matt's face hardened. 'Look, all I'm saying is hold fire a little bit longer before you go rushing into anything.'

There was a moment's silence; it enveloped us and I sat there gazing into space reflecting on what Matt had said.

'It can't be all doom and gloom, I said meekly.' I think Matt saw my helplessness, my dejection, my search for an answer, my search for hope and he made a tentative attempt to make things better.

'I've been in this job just on twelve years and in all that time I think there have been two kids that have left in what I would term, as a positive way. He stood up and put his hand on my shoulder. 'It's out of our hands Jerry lad.'

On the wall, caught in the broken sunlight was a poster showing a child happy, laughing, riding a merry-go round and being held onto by a foster mother. She was smiling, caught up in the child's joy. Underneath were the words: *Every Child Matters.*

Chapter 8

After my talk with Matt I decided to take some leave, clear my head. After one week I returned determined to hold onto the positive. My first handover back tested my resolve. I was told Charlie and Eddy had been involved in a spate of petty crimes, from shoplifting to getting a taxi back to the home in the early hours and then running off without paying the fare.

The shoplifting resulted in a caution from the police and the taxi driver was paid in full by Carol out of petty cash. Charlie and Eddy would pay back the £7.30 between them out of their pocket money. The taxi driver was more than happy to go along with this, as he just wanted his money.

On Wednesday morning I went upstairs collecting all the plates and cups I could find to be washed. I discovered a television and a DVD player were missing from the home. The feeling from staff was that this was the work of Eddy and

Charlie. More worrying, for me, was the rumour that Eddy had introduced Charlie to cocaine. There was no proof but a few of the kids were saying it was true.

Charlie was up and out of bed by 11:30. He looked like shit. He wore only track suit bottoms, which, less than a week old, already had small pot burns in them. His feet were bare, his face sunken. His eyes looked blank and he smelt. He stood there with his hands down the front of his track suit bottoms before greeting me in his usual bright manner.

'Alright, Jerry lad, how's it going?'

I looked him up and down. 'Charlie, what's going on? Why are you getting yourself into all this trouble? You carry on like this and you'll end up locked up.'

Charlie stood there stoned.

'Will yer get us some breakfast, *please?*'

'What do you want?'

I reached into my pocket for the keys before leading the way into the kitchen.

'Open this please.'

He nodded towards the pantry. Charlie surveyed the top shelf, deciding if today was a Rice Krispie day or a Coco Pops day.

'Charlie, you look like shit. Are you okay?'

He nodded, coughing violently into his hand.

'If you keep up this sort of behaviour you're going to go down sooner or later. Do you think Eddy gives a shit about what happens to you?'

'Me and Eddy are gonner get a flat together when we leave here,' he said, shrugging his shoulders before stuffing assorted biscuits and crisps into his track suit bottoms.

'Charlie, why do you all do that?' I said. 'It's not like you're starving, you have a cook that does the loveliest meals and food on tap and you still steal. Why?'

He looked at me with a mischievous grin. The hum of the extractor fan blaring out its monotonous tone was giving me a headache.

'Just supplies Jerry lad, just supplies for munchies time.'

I really should have stopped him, done something, but what was the point? If he didn't do it today it would only happen later. Instead I changed tack.

'What's this about a telly and DVD player going missing, was that you and Eddy?'

Again Charlie flashed a mischievous grin, but this time he nodded confirming what everyone already suspected.

'Charlie,' I said despairingly, 'What the fuck are you doing? Look, you're going have to come clean and do the right thing. This isn't just your home. It's the home of all the other kids too.'

I leaned over and flicked the extractor switch and the fan groaned to a halt.

'You're just robbing off yourself, can't you see that?'

Charlie shrugged his shoulders whilst he fiddled with one of the knobs on the large industrial cooker.

I should have shopped him there and then. Reported it to Matt, but I still held out hope for Charlie and I'd not forgotten what he'd done for me when he placed his poster over the wall I'd brutally punched. I stood there, arms folded, before I asked my next question: 'Some of the kids are saying you're using cocaine. Is that true? Is that why you took the telly and DVD player?'

Charlie stopped twiddling the knobs on the cooker and gave me his full attention. 'Who said that?'

'It doesn't matter who said it, is it true?'

'No,' he said, wiping his nose with the back of his hand. 'No it's not true.'

I knew that this was an important moment in our relationship. I knew Charlie trusted me. What I needed was some kind of bargaining tool in order to get him back on the straight and narrow. Some sort of carrot.

His school placement had become unsustainable and there was talk of putting Charlie into an alternative teaching programme. IMPRESS was the name the council had given to their alternative pathway for kids that dropped out of mainstream school. In reality it meant sitting off and playing pool all day. Staff, amongst themselves, called it Donkey School. Most kids in care eventually ended up at IMPRESS.

Charlie, in the past, had been sporty, but since coming into care despite encouragement from staff, his sporting life had slipped till it was non- existent. Occasionally I would bring in a few boxing DVDs and Charlie would sit for hours watching classic Ali. Charlie was enthralled and asked me if, one day, I might help him find a boxing club. Now seemed the right time.

'Look, remember I said that I would take you to a boxing club I know of?'

Charlie nodded.

'Well how about this Monday? I'm not working, but would come down and pick you up.'

Charlie thought about this for a moment and then said: 'Could little Sammy come as well?'

'I don't see why not, but I would have to clear it with the manager first.'

Charlie seemed elated, suddenly energised. Playfully jabbing me in the shoulder he raised his arms above his head in victory declaring, 'I'm the greatest,' while attempting the Ali shuffle.

'I will also just have to clear it with your key worker, Alan.'

‘I hate that big fuck.’

‘Don’t be like that.’

‘Can’t I have you as a key worker?’

‘It doesn’t work like that.’

‘Why can’t I choose me own key worker?’

‘Cos every kid would want to do the same and before you know it some staff would have loads of key kids and others wouldn’t have any.’

‘So what?’

‘Alan’s okay. You just need to work with him and not against him.’

‘He’s a tit and I don’t like him and I just know he doesn’t like me.’

Charlie was right, but as much as I wanted to agree with the kid I had to be professional.

‘Do you reckon you could take him in a fight, huh? He’s big.’ Charlie flicked out another jab and danced to the side.

I flicked back a playful right hand and tapped him on the top of his head. ‘It’s not all about size boy, it’s about speed and timing.’

Charlie smiled, a big happy smile, one that lit up his whole face. I put my arm around his shoulders and guided him towards the door.

'Right let's go Rocky. Afternoon breakfast is over.'

*

I picked Charlie and little Sammy up Monday evening. As I was not insured to take the kids in my own car I used the home's minibus. Mavis came along in case things didn't go according to plan. I'd spoken with the boxing coach on the Sunday so he knew what to expect. The boxing club would be a different environment, a place with rules and discipline. I always thought of boxing as the great leveller, as no matter how tough someone thought they were there was always somebody tougher. I hoped the boxing would give Charlie a sense of purpose and that he might stop using drugs and stop smoking and be more like the kid he was when I first met him.

The boxing club was situated underneath a pub in what amounted to no more than a cramped basement. A single bulb lit the entrance. The stench of stale sweat hit our nostrils as we entered. Hanging from steel rafters were four punch bags. Three full length mirrors covered the far wall where the boxers could watch themselves whilst they shadow boxed. Even with the lights on there were corners of the gym that remained in the shadows. A few of the lads stared at Charlie and little Sammy as they entered, checking them over, weighing them up. Charlie looked nervous and I winked at him mouthing, 'Don't worry, it'll be alright.'

Once changed into his kit he seemed more relaxed and even managed a smile.

The session went well and Charlie certainly tried his best. At the end of the lesson he threw up, much to the delight of little Sammy. Little Sammy didn't take part, he stood against the wall, arms folded, watching. Afterwards, Macca, the coach, took Charlie to one side and said:

'Look kid you've got some potential, but unless you stop taking all that shit you're no good to me.'

Macca had done his bit, like we'd arranged. I figured perhaps coming from someone else, a stranger outside the home it may reach Charlie.

When I got out to the minibus Charlie and little Sammy were waiting with Mavis. Mavis was comforting Charlie who was crying.

'What's wrong?' I asked, looking at Mavis.

Mavis reached into her pocket and handed Charlie a piece of tissue.

'Charlie, what's wrong?' I asked.

'I…I just can't do it, Jerry. I'm…I'm fucked up,' he sobbed.

'Charlie you're bound to be tired the first time,' said Mavis.

But I knew Charlie meant something far deeper. He was in that dark place that crept up on him when he was alone at night. Emotionally he couldn't engage with the world outside of care and here in a moment of rare clarity, Charlie, knew the battle was lost. I felt a deep sense of sadness followed by an overwhelming anger. I felt I had let Charlie down, failed him. Later, little Sammy told me Charlie threw up because before he went to the gym he'd been so nervous he smoked a spliff.

Charlie never returned to boxing and we never spoke about it again. When the other kids asked, 'How did Charlie do?' I told them he did good.

That night, when I got home, I slipped quietly into Millie's room. She was sleeping, breathing in rhythm, lost in her dreams. I kissed her, gently, on the forehead, a father's promise of eternal love.

*

Alan looked rough. His eyes were puffy and he was sniffing up.

'A touch of cold,' he said when Mavis asked.

I heard the sound of raised voices as I walked towards the kitchen, my hands full of cups I'd collected from the kid's rooms. I looked through the glass and there was Alan, little Sammy and Eddy. Alan was pointing and saying something to Eddy who was waving a pan around like a football flag.

I put the cups onto the side and dug in my pocket for keys. At first, in my haste, I got the wrong key. Finally I opened the door.

'Get out. We don't need you here,' said Eddy through gritted teeth to Alan.

'Yeah, get out,' mirrored little Sammy.'

'I can't leave you unsupervised in the kitchen you know that.' Alan's puffy red eyes blinked behind his glasses. He took out a hanky and wiped his nose. His whole face looked overheated.

'What's going on?' I said.

Alan turned towards me and was about to speak when Eddy moved up beside him and let out a loud fart.

Little Sammy burst into laughter.

'You dirty bastard,' said Alan.

I couldn't believe what I'd just heard. To my mind it sounded like it was said in jest but Alan never jested.

There was a shelf to the right of Eddy. Eddy reached up and took down a bottle of Salad Cream and in large vicious strokes squeezed the contents over the front of Alan's shirt.

'Twat,' said Alan.

Little Sammy was curled up in a tight ball on the floor laughing.

Eddy stepped forward and pushed Alan on the left shoulder, 'Who are you calling a twat, yer cunt.'

I placed myself between them. Eddy did his best to get round me. Alan was staring in disbelief at his shirt. Gradually he became aware of Eddy's anger. Alan's professional button finally kicked in and he strode, hurriedly, towards the door, Eddy and little Sammy in pursuit. Little Sammy shouting, 'Get him Eddy, get him.'

For twenty minutes Eddy banged on the office door shouting that he was going to 'fucking kill' Alan. He only stopped when he thought the police had been called.

*

Alan was wiping himself with a paper towel. There were several used ones crumpled up sitting in the bin. He looked like a statue covered in pigeon shit.

'Are you okay?' I asked.

'Yes. We will have to fill out an incident form.'

I went over to the computer and switched it on. 'Listen Alan, Eddy's asked for a complaints form.'

Alan crushed up the paper towel, swallowed and for a moment closed his eyes. 'Give him one,' he said, his voice low and strained.

*

I wasn't a fan of Alan but I defended him saying that although he'd sworn at Eddy I was sure he never meant anything by it.

He was clearly upset by Eddy's behaviour and it just came out. It was no use, the words of Eddy and little Sammy carried far more weight than my own and Alan lost his job.

As for the rest of us the message from the top brass was clear: 'These are the kids we're working with,' said Victoria Gray, the resource manager.

Eddy just laughed when the news broke that Alan wouldn't be coming back. 'At least it was diet Salad Cream,' he said.

Shortly after Alan's dismissal I took over as Charlie's key worker. It was not formally announced, just expected.

*

There was an advert in the local rag advertising for foster carers.

'Make a Difference' the advert exclaimed.

'You know I think it would be nice,' said Kate.

I gave her an enquiring look, smiling at her. *'Nice'* is a word she knew I always found amusing. It was the word she used to describe me when we first met. Like most men I would have preferred handsome, good-looking or charismatic – but nice…

'Your mother's nice. The little old lady down the street is nice,' I said.

'I mean,' she said, playfully, slapping me on the arm, 'have you given any more thought about bringing Charlie to stay with us?'

'What about Millie?' I said. 'This is no little kid. This is a fifteen-year-old lad.'

'It would do Millie good, an older brother to look up to. I thought you liked Charlie?'

'I do like the kid. I like him a lot but it's a massive step. You have to be careful it's not just some romantic notion about a poor orphan child. The reality is Charlie is a kid with some big issues.'

Kate's dark eyes widened and when she spoke it was almost like an apology. 'He could be the son you'll never have.'

'For fuck's sake, behave yourself.' I placed my hand on her knee. 'It's nothing to do with that,' I said gently. 'I just feel sorry for the kid that's all.'

Kate looked up happy now.

'He has a family,' I said. 'They just need to work things through.'

It's funny but we all think we can save someone and whilst I had a real connection with Charlie, I now knew that wasn't enough to make him change his ways.

'All I'm saying is for the first time we have a little money and if we can help why not?' Kate said.

'I'm not Jesus.'

Kate's face hardened. She picked up the newspaper and began flicking through the pages. 'No one said you were.'

'Look, all I'm saying is that it's not all suffer the little children.'

Kate put down the newspaper and gave me a puzzled look.

'What?' I said gently.

'Nothing, it just doesn't sound like you, 'suffer the little children.''

'Let's just see how things go, okay?' I said, sounding more annoyed than I intended.

'Okay, I just meant…'

'I know what you meant and it's really kind….really nice. All I'm saying is care's not like Oliver Twist anymore. It's moved on.'

I sounded like Matt and I hadn't even been in the job for half the time. Admittedly working in a kid's home was not exactly what I thought it was going to be but what is when you get up close?

***

Chapter 9

Charlie and Eddy found themselves up before the youth court for one of their more inventive ideas. They had gone door to door raffling a teddy bear for Children in Need and then pocketed the donations.

After court Charlie and Eddy bounced into the home in a happy mood.

'What yer get?' asked little Sammy.

'Nine month Supervision Order. I'm not fuckin going, they can shove it,' replied Eddy. He screwed up the paperwork the court had given him and threw it at little Sammy. Charlie did the same with his before following Eddy upstairs. I picked up the papers and filed them.

The warning from the Youth Offending Team (YOT) was a clear one. If they didn't attend their appointments they would be breached and taken back to court for a more severe punishment. The first morning they were due to attend supervision they refused to get out of bed. I telephoned their YOT worker and gave him the news.

'They're just not moving, I've explained that they could be breached but they don't seem bothered,' I said.

The YOT worker thanked me for phoning and then said, 'Perhaps we should think about afternoon appointments for them from now on. Do you have a diary there?'

'Yes.'

'Okay. I'm looking at next Thursday two o' clock.'

I wrote down the time. 'I will let them know,' I said. I thanked him and hung up.

That weekend Eddy and Charlie flagged down a taxi and after telling the driver to pull over a few yards from Acorn House ran off with the driver's takings. The driver easily traced them as he remembered seeing them standing outside smoking when he had picked other kids up from the home.

'What were you thinking, boys?' said Matt.

They both gave a little shrug.

'Have you still got the money?' said Matt.

'Spent it on pot,' said Eddy wiping his eyes with the back of his sleeve and sniffling.

Matt ignored the show of emotion.

'Charlie, this man had to work for that money,' I said nodding towards the taxi driver.

Charlie kept his head down.

The taxi driver's face had softened once Eddy had started getting upset. He ran a hand through his receding hair. 'Look, I don't want to press any charges, I just want my money back. I'd only been out a few hours so call it fifty quid and we can forget about it,' he said.

Eddy's face brightened, a slight grin breaking out but he still dabbed at his eyes.

Charlie looked up happy.

Matt spoke to Carol and she said that the driver could be reimbursed but that YOT had to be informed. I contacted the YOT worker and he agreed with the outcome saying to have pressed charges would only have served to criminalise Charlie and Eddy further.

*

No matter what I tried with Charlie nothing seemed to shift him from his path of destruction.

My despair grew stronger everyday like an aggressive virus.

I told Carol that Charlie's behaviour worried me. She was sensitive to what I was going through and offered me some advice. 'Don't over think things, Jerry. Concentrate on the things you can change, giving the kids nice birthdays and Christmases, spending time with them and being supportive in difficult times.' Perhaps she was right. At the end of the day it was not like Charlie or any of them were my kids.

'The impact you have on a child's life may not be known until years later when the child, as an adult, looks back and recognises what you tried to do for them. Until then all you can do is offer choices and let them make up their own minds,' said Carol.

She was half-right. The trouble was, the kids always made the wrong choices. It wasn't only what was happing to Charlie, other things were happening that made me start to question the sanity of the care system.

*

Zoey was thirteen, a recent admission. She was taken into care because her mother couldn't keep her safe or cope with her behaviour. Zoey had stopped going to school and at night went out partying, using cocaine and an assortment of drugs. Every night would follow the same pattern. Zoey would phone a taxi and off she would go, not returning for three or four days. When she did return home she would sleep all day, recuperate and then the pattern would start again.

She was delicate like a porcelain doll with blonde hair and striking blue eyes. Her skin, surprisingly unblemished despite her appetite for drugs, was a brilliant white. She was so thin you wondered if it was healthy. She was a dainty little thing but full of turmoil and capable of great rage. After her first night in care Zoey went missing for three days.

*

I checked the clock in the hall it showed 10:15pm, but when I checked my watch it was only 9:45pm.

'Is that clock ever right, Margaret?' I asked.

'The kids take the batteries out all the time love, God knows why.'

'I was fifteen minutes closer to going home before my hopes were dashed.'

Margaret laughed. 'No such luck, love.'

It was supper time and so we did the rounds asking each kid what they wanted. I was buttering toast and dividing it onto plates. Margaret carried a plate of toast in one hand and a bowl of Coco-Pops in the other. I opened the door for her and followed behind.

'Here you go, Sammy love,' she said, placing his toast and cereal in front of him.

'How about you honey, you having any supper, Zoey?'

'Don't want any. I'm going out.'

'Zoey, love it's coming up to ten and you said you were staying in tonight.'

Zoey looked at Margaret, nibbled the corner of the toast and pulled a disapproving face. 'This tastes shit. It's burnt.'

Margaret let out a deep sigh. 'I can make you some more.'

'I'm going out,' said Zoey. 'I'll get something to eat when I'm out—some decent food, a Maccies.'

Zoey stood up, pushing her chair back. Her mobile phone chimed with an incoming message. A smile of delight broke across her young face, as she read the message. 'Right, I'm off, they'll be here in a mo.'

Shelly came out of the office and shot me and Margaret a look. I nodded indicating Zoey was about to do one.

'And where do you think you're going young lady?' asked Shelly.

'Out,' Zoey answered, flatly. 'You can't stop me.'

To stand in her way and physically attempt to stop her would be futile. She might put a chair through a window and jump out and injure herself. It was always a dilemma because if a child was injured you could find yourself before the authority justifying every step you had taken. You could lose your job.

A month before I had been sent on compulsory THINK FIRST training. This was a three day session with second rate actors playing the parts of kids in care and I have to say, it was all cleverly done, especially around the concept of ‘challenging behaviour.’

*

It was 9:15am when I got there. Lunch was already laid out.

The staff from other homes drifted in and got themselves a coffee from the machine, greeting other workers they only got to see at training events, while the smokers nipped outside for a quick cigarette before the session began. I spotted Tom, a worker from another home I’d met some weeks before during a domestic violence workshop. He came straight over and handed me a cup of coffee.

‘Alright, mate.’

‘Hello, Tom. How are you?’

‘I’m fine thanks.’

He took a sip of his coffee. ‘How’s things at Acorn House these days mate?’

‘Same old shit.’

‘Same in our place mate, it never changes, only the faces.’

I nodded and took a sip of coffee. The sweetness of it surprised me. I didn’t take sugar, but decided not to say anything. After all it was nice of Tom to get me the drink.

'So, what's all this about?' said Tom.

'Handling challenging behaviour I was told, or as Matt calls it, Social Services insurance policy so if you do get twatted they can say, well we gave you the training you must not have applied it properly.'

'Is right,' said Tom.

*

'Hello, my name is Gavin and I would like to welcome you all here today for ours and your THINK FIRST training.'

Gavin stopped and moved lightly to the back of the room indicating a Power Point screen showing the steps to the use of physical restraint.

A GUIDE TO THE USE OF PHYSICAL RESTRAINT

Ascertain that the circumstances meet the Restraint criteria-Risk of Serious Harm

Caution the child orally that Physical Restraint Will take place unless the behaviour stops

It is important that other staff Are present-to support or act as witness

Use only minimum force to avert injury or harm

Notify Home's Manager without delay and the Social Worker ASAP

Complete Critical Incident form ASAP, within 48 hours and inform the Resource Manager

Write up Additional Measures of Control Book-signed by Home Manager

Supervision by Home's Manager no later than 24 Hours

Events should be discussed in team Meetings.

Episode should be discussed with the in key work sessions with child/ren

Gavin picked up his bottled water and took a short drink. 'Now before I introduce our fine bunch of actors sitting behind me...'

We all stared at the actors. Two lads and three girls not yet out of their adolescence smiled back, warm inclusive smiles.

'...I would like to tell you about the purpose of the next three days and what we hope to achieve. We provide, *approved,* physical intervention and harm reduction training techniques that you can add to the *toolbox* of your already existing work practices.' Gavin held up his index fingers drawing imaginary speech marks in the air around the word *'toolbox.'*

'All of you here deal, on a daily basis, with challenging behaviour and today and over the next two days we're going to instruct you on a number of different physical intervention techniques such as, *buffering, blocking, basic cradle holds and prevention of self-harm.* All these terms will become familiar over the next few days, when they will be demonstrated by this dishevelled lot.'

He indicated the actors with a jerk of his thumb over his shoulder. A murmur of light laughter trickled around the room and the actors did their best to look offended.

Gavin was light on his feet, his slender frame perspiring with effort, droplets of sweat on his bald head. He had spent the last five minutes using his tall frame to block a doorway to prevent one of the male actors from leaving the building, positioning his body sideways in the door frame, hands outstretched, left leg used as an anchor of support against the young actor's best efforts whilst continuing to talk the young person down. A demonstration of physical intervention and Gavin was clearly out of breath. 'It's tough when you get into your early thirties.'

We all laughed because Gavin was at least in his early forties. We all took turns door blocking. When it came to my turn I was paired with a woman of about fifty-five. I didn't try too hard.

After morning break the actors performed a short scene: 'Right here,' said Gavin. 'Sian our lovely young actress,' Sian did a playful curtsy to us, 'will now play a young person aged about fifteen who hasn't been out of her room for three days and has eaten very little. Now, enter, Bill, our handsome male lead.' Bill not to be left out gave an ostentatious bow to the audience. 'Bill is a carer who has just come on shift, sees Sian sitting on the sofa, out of her room, and speaks to her trying to get to the heart of Sian's challenging behaviour.'

Bill went into action. 'Hi, Sian honey, have not seen you for a long time. How are you?' Sian stared ahead, sucking her thumb, legs tucked under her body. 'Have you had something to eat? Would you like me to get you something?' Sian didn't answer. 'I tell you what, perhaps we can watch some TV later or go out to the cinema, how about that?' Sian continued to stare into space. Bill was about to speak when Gavin interrupted.

'Okay. Let's freeze it there.' Gavin turned towards us. 'Any suggestions?'

'I actually think that she's communicating a lot. Although she's not saying anything verbally her body language is communicating a lot. I think she wants to talk otherwise she would still be in her room.' It was someone from one of the other homes, someone I didn't know.

'Yes, yes, good,' said Gavin. 'Remember, all behaviour is communication.'

People nodded in agreement, but this was certainly not my idea of challenging behaviour. This type of behaviour I could do all fucking night. Gavin continued, 'Okay. Would someone like to come forward and be the carer and we will pick the scene up from where we left it?'

And so it went on: Scene, freeze, scene, and freeze.

We then had the actors playing a scene where a kid gets angry because his father cancels a visit and the kid, upset, smashes up his room before a worker can calm him down. Next a scene where a kid wouldn't get out of bed for school and the worker talked the child round. When asked what we, as carers, would do, one employee raised an objection.

'What can you do if they don't want to go to school? You can't drag them out the bed. They'd put in a complaint.'

Gavin quickly shuffled on.

More scenes, endless scenes but we had no scenes where a kid smashed up your car or spat in your face.

*

The second day consisted of different holds being demonstrated by the actors, holds designed to nullify a situation without bending joints or risking any injury to the child. Then we tried them out on each other. Again, I could easily have resisted, as the woman I was paired with had very little strength, but there seemed little point.

*

The third day was a combination of days one and two. By now people were bored. The review of days one and two was a good thing because people had forgotten how to do the holds. Someone asked if they could be a challenging child and Gavin try to restrain them but Gavin said no.

'I'm afraid to restrain in case the child makes an allegation,' said a woman from one of the other homes. She looked around the room for support. Slowly, people began to speak up, protesting they too were afraid to restrain because of allegations.

Gavin defended his livelihood. 'You have a right to restrain using the *correct* methods.'

Then someone asked Gavin if he or any of his group had ever worked in care. Gavin told us that neither he nor any of the actors had worked in care but had done extensive research.

'What kind of research?' Tom asked. He sat forward and studied Gavin.

Gavin pulled at the tip of his nose. 'We've done a large amount of reading.'

'Oh, reading,' said Tom, sitting back in his chair.

A light ripple of laughter went round the room. On that day we finished early. Evaluation forms were handed out. I sat contemplating what score to give the last few days. I found myself thinking, not for the first time, out of all the training workshops I had attended, how many of the people charged with equipping us to do our job better would swap places with us?

'Once we've filled out our evaluation forms can we go?' someone asked.

'Yes,' said Gavin.

*

'Yes! They're here,' said Zoey, heading for the front door. Shelly placed her body in the door frame *blocking* Zoey's path whilst gently *buffering* her away from the door.

'Get out of my fucking way,' said Zoey.

'You know we can't let you out,' said Shelly.

'Fuck you.'

Time seemed to stand still, but not in the way I wished. There was no freezing of the scene to discuss options, although I wished we could. I cautiously approached Zoey.

'Come on, Zoey, be sensible.' If what I said had any impact on Zoey it was broken by the sound of a car horn. The other kids quickly gathered for the show.

'Let her go. You can't stop her,' it was Bethany with the truth.

'Stay out of it, Bethany,' shouted Margaret and looked shocked by the anger in her own voice.

I closed in. I Checked Shelly's body language for a clue of what came next, a *cradle hold* perhaps or *guiding the client gently by the arm.*

'Fuck off,' said Zoey.

Within a micro second she'd broken away from Shelly, was out the door and ran towards the waiting car.

'Jerry, go after her. See if you can get the registration of the car.'

Yeah thanks for that Shelly, I thought.

'Zoey, hold on,' I said. 'Don't go with them.'

'Fuck off, Jerry.'

I got to the car, Zoey was already inside. It had been a long time since I'd run and the cold air hurt the back of my throat. There were four men aged maybe 22, 25. I couldn't quite tell in the light. The one next to the driver spoke. 'What's up mate?' A large knife rested in his lap. I tried not to look afraid.

'That girl,' I said. 'She's only 13 and this is a children's home.'

The lad shrugged.

'I'm just letting you know, as soon as you drive away the police will be called and your registration given.'

He sniffed, and then sniffed again. 'Laughin,' what yer wanner do Zoey?' he said.

'Just go in, Jerry. I can do what I want'

She was right. I looked back to Shelly, Margaret and the kids standing on the step. 'Fine, I'm just telling you the police will be called. You're taking a minor out and you need to be aware that–' the car was gone, its engine roaring like it was on a race track.

*

'Take a look at this.' Mavis handed me a sheet of paper.

57 fucks

107 sucks

'Is this yours?' I said laughing.

'Poor kid, its Zoey's. I did a key worker session with her and brought up the subject of sexual health and that she should think about getting checked out for any diseases. That's her list of sexual partners.'

I looked at the scribbled writing again but this time with the gravity it deserved. 'Will she go?'

'She's refused. She's sleeping with these men for money and drugs,' said Mavis gravely.

'Offer her something,' I said, 'an activity, the cinema.'

'I have but she's not biting. I'm going to call her social worker, she'll have to do something. This can't go on. I mean she's only thirteen.'

*

A Specific Issues meeting was called and shortly after that, a Sexual Exploitation meeting and finally a Strategy meeting.

The meetings all ended the same way. 'I think the best way for us to proceed is to monitor the situation whilst offering Zoey alternatives in the form of structured activities,' management would say.

One such activity was a week away at Pontins.

Mavis asked if I would go with her and Zoey. It meant I had to sleep on a sofa bed but I said yes, hoping the time away would help the kid trust us more. I would do three days and then Matt would take over.

Evenings were the worst, as Zoey would get restless not being used to the change in her routine. It wasn't easy but we did our best to keep her entertained. She liked ice cream and we indulged her by allowing three a day.

Zoey loved the magic show, her eyes lit up when the magician produced a white dove from under his top hat. 'Can I have a bird?' she asked. 'I could keep it in me room.'

Mavis smiled. 'Oh, I'm sorry love we can't have pets at the home.'

'Why?' Zoey said, hurt.

Mavis shot me a look. 'Health and safety, babe, isn't that right, Jerry?'

'Yes, I said, 'rules are rules.'

'Stupid,' said Zoey, turning back to the magician who had just produced another two fluttering doves from his hat. Zoey clapped enthusiastically.

'Can you imagine pets at our place?' said Mavis in a hushed voice to me. 'The little buggers would kill them.'

Zoey screamed with approval along with all the other kids when the magician asked if he should put his lovely assistant in the box and drive large swords into her.

We went back to our chalet that evening all smiles, Zoey clutching a large white stuffed rabbit. After standing outside for her last cigarette of the night she went to bed.

*

The next morning we took Zoey to the adventure pool. I sat with Mavis at poolside and drank tea while Zoey attacked the slides with zest. We nearly hadn't gone when Mavis saw the swimming costume Zoey had packed.

'You're not wearing that. A girl of your age showing yourself off that way,' said Mavis tutting.

'For fuck's sake,' screamed Zoey smashing her breakfast bowl on the floor.

Outside our chalet window, on the grass, was a woman with two small boys playing cricket. I watched as the woman looked over towards our window. After a moment of brief consideration, she picked up the wickets and shouted at the boys to move further away out of ear shot.

It was only with the promise of ice cream later and £3.50 cash in hand for sweets that Zoey relented.

'What if I spend it on bifftas?' Zoey said, her voice calm.

'I never heard that,' said Mavis. 'Did you Jerry?'

I shook my head. It was a necessary compromise and one that would stop Zoey asking strangers for a spare biffta.

Mavis picked out a respectable bathing suit at the pool and bought it. These little temper tantrums were expected but always ended in smiles.

There were times when the kid's insight was far beyond her years and she would tell us she knew what she was doing was wrong.

'I just wish they would lock me up, I don't know why I shag and do drugs. I just do.'

'Then change, said Mavis softly. 'We'll help you, if you'll let us.'

Zoey brushed her hair from her eyes. 'I can't.' There was a certainty in her reply, as if the thing she was hiding from would never let her rest.

After the pool we had lunch. The sun had made an appearance so we walked the short distance to the beach, badminton set in hand.

Our first day back home, Zoey went missing for three days. For me the only answer was to secure her while some therapeutic work could be done. Reporting her missing to the social worker I voiced this opinion and was harshly told, 'To place her in secure would be punishing her when she's the victim. It's the horrible men that are supplying her with drugs and then having sex with her that should be punished.'

*

When the opportunity presented itself I pressed Carol.

'Jerry, to secure Zoey, would be an infringement of her rights,' said Carol.

'Does that include the child's right to prostitute herself?' I asked, my voice taut.

Carol let out a long, laboured breath.

'I think you're being a little too simplistic,' she said, smiling. 'Like it or not there are procedures to follow and if they're not followed any judge would ask what alternatives had been explored. If all alternatives had been tried, but failed then the judge *might* consider secure. This is not like securing a child who has committed a crime against society.'

'I guess it's not cheap either?'

Carol sat down and indicated for me to do likewise. 'To secure a child isn't cheap. It costs a lot more than keeping her here.'

For a moment I just looked at Carol. I was sure she already knew what my next question was going to be but I asked it anyway. 'So what happens, God forbid, if the kid ends up dead whilst Social Services *explore* all the alternatives? What would the judge say then?'

'Then I would have to stand up in court and when the judge asked what we did, I would have to show that everything possible in our power had been done, one-on-one activities, time away and so forth.' She opened a drawer and took out Zoey's client diary file adding gravity to her words. 'That's why it's so important to log every piece of information.'

'Yeah well, just because a kid has the rights doesn't always make those rights right,' I said.

She stood up and placed the file back in the drawer. ‘No it doesn’t, but that’s not my or your decision. We just have to keep on keeping on, for Zoey.’

***

Chapter 10

The relationship between Charlie and his adoptive mother was strained to say the least. They seldom spoke but when they did it was as if each was going through the motions.

'How's he been?' she would ask.

I would oblige and bring her up to date on Charlie's current list of convictions and she would do her best to look sad and say, 'Terrible, just terrible.' We would both stand there, me playing the part of the sympathetic worker to her loss when in reality I was thinking *you heartless bitch.* But perhaps I was being unfair on the mother simply because it was her that dealt with Social Services and not the father. This childless couple must have always wanted children. I mean why else would they adopt?

Even when a financial assessment was carried out and it was deemed Charlie's parents must contribute to his up-keep they did not balk. The only time they became vocal was at the prospect of their child returning home. The father remained detached and, it seemed, even more untouched by Charlie's predicament than the mother.

He was not here this day. He was busy clearing out the attic. As we stood by her car, the black bin bag containing some more of Charlie's belongings at her feet, I sensed in the mother an urgency to be gone.

'Are you our Charlie's mum?' asked Bethany approaching us. Bethany smelt of stale piss. I could see from the look on Charlie's mother's face that she too was overcome by the stench, but we both tried to pretend we didn't notice.

'Get yourself in Beth,' I said. 'We're talking about some important, private, stuff here.'

Little Sammy appeared with a cigarette and Bethany ambled away towards him. 'Sammy save us on yer biffta!' she shouted.

She had run out of cigarettes and wouldn't be visiting her mother till Friday.

Charlie's mother opened the car door when Charlie, drawn by the cigarette, made an appearance and spotted his mum. He came over smiling and I could see the mother was caught.

'Hi Mum, how's things?'

Charlie's mother hesitated and took the key out of the ignition. 'Fine, Charlie, how are you?'

'Okay,' he sniffed.

His mother looked him over and her eyes stopped on the cigarette in Charlie's hand. Charlie moved to put the cigarette behind his back in a half-hearted attempt to hide his sin, perhaps out of some old reflex or a sign of respect, but the smoke refused to be hid and drifted up and away dissolving into nothing.

'Is Amanda alright? I want to get up and see her.'

'Yes. She's fine. I'll ask your Dad when you can come up. I'll ring you and let you know. It's just that we have a lot on this week.'

Charlie went for it, but I could tell he'd been given the brush off. Perhaps they were worried, Charlie had begun asking too many questions about his birth mother and he might mention it to Amanda. They were having no trouble with Charlie's sister and perhaps they wanted to keep it that way. I knew I shouldn't, but I couldn't resist and there was a part of me that was enjoying the mother's uneasiness.

'If Charlie rings you and we arrange a day, I can drive Charlie up and pick up Amanda and they could go the cinema or something together. It's no trouble.'

The mother glared at me and I knew I'd hit a home run. She reached down to put the key in the ignition and started the car. 'Okay that would be nice. Take care, Charlie, I have to dash, I told Dad I wouldn't be long,' she said, closing the car door.

Charlie grabbed the handle and opened the door before she could pull away. 'Mum, have yer got three quid so I can get a magazine?'

The mother hesitated before reaching for her purse and handing Charlie three pounds. Charlie closed the car door and tapped the glass indicating for his mother to wind the window down.

'See yer when yer bring the rest of me stuff and tell Amanda I'll see her soon.'

The car moved away, Charlie and the mother waving goodbye. We stood there for a moment contemplating the bin bag.

'Do us a favour, Jerry, lad. Take the bag up to me room.'

'No probs.'

Eddy came out onto the front step and he and Charlie headed for the local shop. I knew the money was going on cigarettes. I picked the bag of clothing up and headed for Charlie's bedroom, another step in the process of the mother and father ridding themselves of all that was Charlie.

'Fancy a kick about when we get back, Jerry lad?' Charlie shouted as he walked away.

'Alright, yeah,' I answered.

He didn't come back.

*

In the days following his mother's visit Charlie seemed a little restless. He looked rough, his eyes were red and he'd lost a little of his bounce.

He'd played it cool with his mother but I knew it was just an act. Charlie was a boy of two mothers and two fathers, a heritage that must have been so difficult for him to come to terms with.

'How do you handle it, Jerry?' he asked me.

'Handle what?'

'Feeling fucked off.'

Such conversations always seemed to happen at bed time, at the time, I guess, the kids are left alone with their thoughts. I slumped down onto the end of Charlie's bed.

'My wife, Kate, and my kid, Millie, that's how I deal with it. Millie's seven now and I guess that's all I need.'

Charlie sat back, his arms behind his head following every word. I'd never revealed anything of my personal life before. I guarded against it on advice from Matt who told me sooner or later one of the little bastards would use it against you, but I felt Charlie was different and while that may have been Matt's experience it didn't mean it applied to everyone.

'You see, I never got on with my mum. She was always for my younger sister, Brenda, still is. Dad's pretty much the same but at least I can talk to him now. It used to really fuck me off, get me down, until Kate came along and little Millie and then everything changed. You know there were times I was treated so different from my sister I began to think I was adopted.' I caught myself. 'Sorry Charlie, I didn't mean it like that.'

'It's okay.'

There was a look in his eyes I'd not seen before, a flicker of emotion, a young kid searching for a sense of belonging.

'Anyway, all I need is Kate and Millie they're my family and that's what counts. One day you'll have your own family and nothing else will mean shit, you'll see.'

Charlie kicked his trainers off using his feet to flick them onto the floor. I recoiled, pretending to faint at the smell.

'Yeah, well one day, I'm gonner find my real mum.'

'I hope you do lad, but don't give up on your family, you might be able to patch it up yet.' I didn't believe this but thought it was the right thing to say.

Charlie looked at me. An amused smile broke across his face, 'If they cared I wouldn't be in here.'

I knew he was right but I said nothing. My silence was taken as agreement. But his birth mother had also given him up albeit, Charlie reasoned, to give him and his sister a better life, equally not a good thing to do but perhaps in his eyes a more worthy one.

It was not long after our talk that the little changes I'd noted in Charlie became more visible. He could be erratic, picking arguments with staff over trivial things like closing his bedroom door when he was out when he wanted it left open. Other times he would be remote and subdued, not communicating with anyone just staying in his room all day only coming out when the other kids were going to bed, then he would slip out and not return till morning.

*

Christmas was a chaotic time in care. Staff put up decorations and worked hard to make the home look jovial. A budget for presents of £300.00 would be allocated to each child. On top of that an extra

£150.00 was given for clothing money. The kids would go shopping with their key worker or make a list and their key workers would do the shopping. Mostly the lists consisted of mobile phones, expensive trainers and jewellery. Everything receipted. Forty pounds was kept back by each key worker to buy surprises for the children. There was seldom any involvement from parents.

Key workers tried to get as many of the children home over the Christmas period as possible but success was limited. Money was given to the children so they could buy presents for their families. I wondered how the kids still living at home must have felt when their brothers and sisters arrived with a bag full of expensive gifts, care of Social Services. It must have sent the message that being in care was a good thing. None of the parents, to my knowledge, contributed any money.

Two months earlier the charity letters were sent out to local businesses and shops reminding them that in this time of giving please spare a thought for those less fortunate. With each donation received Margaret would cheer.

'Great! Pantomime tickets,' or 'Wonderful! Vouchers for W.H. Smiths. Fantastic.' But it's wasn't all wonderful news and with every rejection letter Margaret would let her disappointment be known, 'Tight *buggers.'*

I stood warming myself on the radiator in the main office, as Margaret recounted to Carol her number of victories for the week.

'So, with the ten pantomime tickets and the food hamper from ASDA and the vouchers for W.H. Smiths we haven't done bad this year.'

Margaret was full of sunshine. Her eyes moved from Carol to Matt then me. I nodded and smiled. I could tell Matt was doing his best to appear interested.

'Excellent work, Margaret, you've done really well,' said Carol. Margaret continued, 'I'll print out a poster and the kids that are interested in the pantomime can put their names down if they want to go. I'll put a note in the communications book for key workers to ask their key child if they're interested in going.'

Carol picked up the signing in sheet and added her signature to the list of staff for the day.

'Margaret, perhaps some of the other donations could be put as stocking fillers for the kids.'

Margaret's face beamed with delight. 'Good idea.'

There was a knock on the door. Bethany's face appeared at the glass.

'Just a minute honey,' Margaret said.

There was a loud crash as Bethany kicked the door. 'Get me some fucking travel money,' she shouted.

'Sweetheart, said Margaret. 'We're not going to get travel with that type of behaviour are we?'

'What's wrong with her this morning?' Carol asked, of no one in particular.

'She was like that last night, very demanding,' said Matt.

'I don't think she's got any cigarettes,' added Margaret.

'That'll be it. That's why she's up early wanting to go to her placement,' said Matt. 'She'll want the travel money for fags. So what do I do?'

Carol thought for a moment. 'I tell you what, just give her a travel pass.'

Matt looked in the petty cash tin. 'We've got none. He thought for a moment and then said, 'I'll have to give her money, but warn her if she doesn't turn up at her placement it'll be taken out of her pocket money.'

Again there was a crash at the door. 'Hurrrrry up,' said Bethany drawing out her voice.

'Make sure she knows the score,' said Matt, handing Margaret Bethany's travel money.

'I'm coming sweetheart,' said Margaret. Carol was about to follow behind and go into her office when she stopped. 'I tell you what. Ask Margaret to drive Bethany to the station and pay her on the train and pick up some travel passes.'

Matt nodded. 'Okay, no probs.'

While Matt made busy checking the petty cash receipts all had signatures I took the opportunity to look through some of the donated items: Two large remote-control cars caught my eye. 'I tell you what, these are a bit of alright, aren't they?'

Matt looked up. 'Spoilt little scum bags, they get fucking everything. I wouldn't mind, but the little bastards don't appreciate anything. There's kids starving in this world with fuck all and these little cunts get everything. I wish I could afford to spend over three hundred quid on each of mine for Christmas.' He paused. When he spoke he chose his words carefully, measuring them so nothing was wasted.

'You see, Jerry, I don't believe in writing begging letters 'cos these little bastards get loads already. More than enough, and they don't appreciate any of it.'

Matt slammed the cash box shut.

'The whole fucking system is built on materialism. The incentives and the rewards are given for the smallest things. Fuck, if a kid put its shoes on the right feet it gets a fiver. I'll tell you something else too'–he was in full flow now–'Margaret can do all she wants, don't get me wrong, she's lovely like, but she won't get any better thought of, not by them little scrotes or by the top brass.'

'The cars are nice though. I wouldn't mind a go of one of these myself.'

'Jerry, they won't last five minutes, trust me.'

Matt placed the petty cash tin back in the safe.

'Last year we got a couple of remote control cars donated to us and little Sammy and Eddy took them out onto the front road and sent them, purposely, into the oncoming cars, laughing whilst they were doing it. That's how much they appreciate stuff. It's just more stuff to sell or break, that's all. It doesn't mean a fuck to them.'

*

Three days later I was alone in the office when a lady called saying she had a donation of toys and wanted to arrange to bring them round for the children in the home. I thanked her but told her we were more than adequately funded by the council. We had been inundated with donations and perhaps she might like to give them to a children's hospice, as I'd heard their only funding came via donations. This, of course, was against protocol but I didn't care. I never told anyone about the call, not even Matt.

Nobody really wanted to work on Christmas day, preferring to be at home with their own kids but I was the newest addition to the team so I had little choice. I worked the Christmas Eve late shift. It turned out it was no different from any other shift except Matt wore a pristine white shirt that made him look even more like Jesus. Charlie went home for Christmas morning but was back by the evening. He also got a Play Station. He sold it two weeks later.

***

Chapter 11

I got home just on two-thirty in the morning, thankful I wasn't on the early shift the following day. I switched on the television, but kept the sound down. I find it's often better that way, its flickering light, the only illumination in the room, always makes me feel at peace. But that night it wasn't having the desired effect. I felt like shit, the gnawing of a thumping headache was getting stronger. Still, I only had myself to blame. If I'd have been a fraction quicker getting my coat I would have been home free. But I couldn't have left Charlie in the state he was in.

At 10:55 pm. Shelly had nodded for me to get off, as all the kids were busy in their rooms watching reality TV. I was zipping my jacket up in the main office when I heard the raised voices of Eddy and Charlie returning.

Charlie stumbled up the stairs while Eddy said, 'He's pissed.' The other kids came out of their rooms and stood on the stairs watching Charlie who began to play to his audience. Throwing his arms around me Charlie sprayed me with a greeting of, 'Alright Jerry lad.' I recoiled from the stench of alcohol.

'Let's get you up to your room Charlie,' I said.

Debbie was trying to get the other kids back into their bedrooms, whilst Shelly and I dealt with Eddy and Charlie. The kids were about to give way and return to their TVs when Eddy shouted, 'Who wants a biffta?' There was a mass movement of bodies, a great exodus, as the kids all headed for the front step. It was nice, I thought, that Eddy had suddenly discovered the concept of sharing, but why this fucking late at night? When this happened there was nothing to do but go with it.

'Make it a quick one you lot. I just had everyone settled for the night before you two came back,' said Debbie, attempting a mock look of anger.

'Can I have some toast *please,* Debbie?' Eddy asked. He seemed in a playful mood so Debbie ran with it.

'When you're in your room and settled.'

Debbie had been night staff a long time and experience had taught her you never promise toast unless they're in their rooms. Finally the kids ambled their way upstairs and to their bedrooms. Eddy put his arm around Debbie.

'A nice cup of tea with that toast, two sugars,' he winked at Debbie.

'Get lost; what did your last slave die from?'

'Not doing as she was told.'

'Go on, in your room and I'll see what I can do.'

I checked my watch, it was coming up to eleven-thirty, enough time to check on Charlie before I left for home. I headed for Charlie's room; he hadn't come down for a cigarette, which was unusual for him; unusual for any of them.

I tapped on Charlie's door,

'Charlie, it's Jerry. You okay?'

'Come in, Jerry lad.' I took my key and opened the door. Charlie lay on the bed, a small electric fan turned towards him on the bedside table moving to and fro like a spectator at Wimbledon.

'Charlie, where have you and Eddy been?' I asked.

'Around town, and then down to the park,' he slurred. I could hear the kids outside being ushered to their rooms, and knew the others had got things under control. I approached the bed and perched myself on the edge.

'Where did you get the drink?'

Charlie looked up and tapped the side of his nose with his finger.

'We have our ways, Jerry lad, we have our ways.'

I shook my head.

'Listen, you haven't just had drink have you?'

'Ave had a bit of bugle.' Bugle was slang for cocaine. The kids had many names for it.

'Charlie, how much stuff have you taken?' I asked, trying to conceal my panic.

'I don't know.' His voice seemed sleepy, as if the effort of talking had spent him.

'Did Eddy have any?'

'Nah, he had some drink, but he just buzzed off me.'

I sat there for a moment, as I needed time to think. Charlie looked completely out of it. The panic began to swell in me. I had to let Shelly know because if any harm came to Charlie I would never forgive myself. I knew Charlie wouldn't thank me for it but it had to be done.

I slipped out of the room and beckoned to Shelly who was busy ferrying toast to each of the kids. I caught her eye.

'Charlie's out of it and he says he's taken coke as well as drink.'

Shelly let out a long sigh and we both moved out of earshot of the other kids.

'He's going to have to go to the hospital.' She paused, as Bethany walked past towards the toilet,

'What about Eddy, did he have any?'

'He says not, but he might not want to grass.'

'You go and talk to him and see if he'll go with Debbie in an ambulance and I'll check if Eddy has had any.'

'What if he won't?'

'Tell him he's no choice.'

I headed back to Charlie's room. He was flat on his back staring up at the ceiling, his face a pasty white. He was sweating and grinding his teeth.

'Charlie,' I said gently shaking him. 'You're going to have to go the hospital, mate.' Charlie was up and at me like a waking tiger.

'What did yer tell for?' he screamed. 'Yer bastard, what did yer tell for?'

I was shocked I'd seen him get angry before, but never at me. 'Charlie, I just want to make sure you're okay, that's all. I didn't mean any harm.'

'Well I'm not fucking going. Yer can all just fuck off.'

'Charlie if you don't go they'll get the police and make you go.'

'I don't care, now fuck off and leave me alone.' He swung round and struck the wardrobe door with his fist and then began headbutting the wall, accompanying each headbutt with the chant, 'Leave me alone, leave me alone, leave me alone.'

I left the room looking for Shelly who along with Debbie had heard the shouting and was already heading in my direction.

'Shelly, he's not having any of it. He says he won't go and he's freaking out.'

All three of us ran to the room, but Charlie had slammed the door. From inside we could hear him smashing up his room and screaming,

'Fuck off, fuck off!'

I put my key in the door, but it wouldn't budge. I got my shoulder behind it and it still wouldn't shift.

'It's no good, Shelly, he's barricaded himself in.'

After a few moments the thrashing and screaming stopped and the three of us stood there listening.

'Is Charlie trippin?' Little Sammy came out of his room to investigate. Getting no reply little

Sammy drew his own conclusion. 'Buzzin, Charlie's sledging,' he said with excitement.

'Come on you, in your room,' said Debbie.

'Can I have a drink first?'

'When you're in your room,' replied Debbie, gently trying to buffer little Sammy towards his bedroom.

'What's up with our Charlie?' It was Bethany, never one to be left out.

'Never mind about Charlie you both get yourselves in bed or there are no drinks for anyone.'

'Charlie, are yer alright lad?' shouted Bethany.

'He's trippin,' laughed little Sammy.

'You'll be trippin in a minute if you don't get to your room,' added Debbie shaking her fist playfully.

'I need a drink,' said Bethany.

'If you all just get to your rooms then you can have a drink,' said Shelly, joining Debbie in an attempt to control the situation.

I bent down to look through the keyhole, but could see nothing, as there was something blocking the view. When I looked up, Michael, a thirteen-year-old who had only come in the night before and was in the room next to Charlie, had come out.

'What's all da noise?' he asked, rubbing his eyes.

'It's nothing,' I said. 'Now go in your room and don't worry about it.'

'But I can't sleep 'cos of da noise.'

'Don't worry about it, I'm sorting it, just go in your room please and close the door.'

'He's not going in his room is he?' he said, nodding at little Sammy who was still enjoying the show despite the best efforts of Debbie and Shelly. My God, I thought, he's only been in a fucking a day and already he's learned the dance, but at that moment the kid was still uncertain, I could see it in his eyes. I sensed it in his demeanour by the way he hovered, hesitant, inside his bedroom door, not quite crossing the threshold.

'Look, get in your room or I'll take your telly,' I said doing my best to sound firm. In another day or two he would know I couldn't take his telly, but for now it worked; he retreated and closed his door. I saw Shelly smiling at me and I gave her a knowing wink.

Shelly sidled up besides me. 'Try and talk him down Jerry, he has a strong relationship with you.'

She gave me a reassuring smile and I smiled back feeling none of the confidence I was attempting to portray.

'Charlie,' I said, in a low tone, trying to put as much warmth into my voice as possible. There was no answer and I gently knocked on the door and again I tried. 'Charlie.' Silence. I put my key in the door, but it still wouldn't shift.

'Charlie, it's Jerry, just let me in. I need to check that you're okay.'

I tried my key again and this time with my shoulder against the door it gave way. I edged the door open enough to allow me to squeeze my body through sideways. The edge of the carpet came up as I did so. Charlie was sitting in the far corner of the room, his head buried in his knees.

'I'm sorry, Jerry lad, I didn't mean it.'

He didn't look up.

'It's okay.' I moved to him and came down on one knee so we were on the same level. 'Charlie, you can't go on this way lad. You're killing yourself.' I could hear the faint whispering of Shelly and Debbie on the other side of the door. Charlie raised his face to me and his eyes seemed vacant and lost. He held out his hand towards me and I could see the knuckles were an angry red where he'd punched the door of the wardrobe. I felt a sense of real pity for him. He looked so helpless and small and it might simply have been that it was late and I was tired, but he suddenly looked a lot older. He seemed worn out.

'Jerry,' he said tearfully, 'can I…can I come and live with you?'

I heard the words but the impact of them went deeper, far deeper.

'Charlie, it wouldn't work lad.'

He looked at me his eyes pleading,

'*Please,* I won't do the drugs and I won't go on the rob no more.'

In that moment I know he saw me as perhaps his last hope, his only saviour. I paused for what felt like an eternity before I answered.

'I can't Charlie…I just can't.' The truth was I did want to take Charlie home, I wanted to protect him and make everything okay, but as a father I was afraid for my own child. I mean how could I subject my child to the drugs, the stealing, the smoking and the drinking? How could anyone?

'Why? I thought yer liked me?'

'I do like you, but I can't take you home.'

'Why?'

Suddenly I felt trapped by the dilemma in front of me. I knew whatever answer I gave, unless it was yes, like everything else in the fucked up care system he would hate me for it. So I did the only thing I could. I did the right thing. I did the honest thing, because at the very least Charlie deserved my honesty.

'I just can't, I've…you know I've got my own kid Charlie and I've seen what happens in here. I've seen kids that don't smoke or do drugs and within a few weeks they're the same as the rest.'

'Yer bastards, yer all the same, just in it for the money.' He stared at me his eyes filling with tears. 'None of yers cares!'

His words angered me. 'Charlie, you're wrong. Do you think me…any of us like taking shit everyday? If it was about money, I could earn money working at ASDA. But I'm not, I'm here, so don't tell me I don't care. I mean look at you Charlie. Look at where you are, look at what you've become, I can't take you home to my child… I'm sorry.'

I felt bad for saying it; he didn't deserve this. Perhaps Charlie was right in what he said; care was just a word we used and I'd been an idiot for thinking otherwise. Matt had warned me that only a fool gets emotionally involved. You had to treat it just like any other job, go home and forget about it.

Charlie began to sob and I put my arm around his shoulder.

'It's okay Charlie, it's okay,' I whispered.

Debbie popped her head round the door. Her eyes went to Charlie and she gave me a sad little smile and then mouthed,

'The ambulance is on its way.' I gave her a nod and she was gone. I leaned forward, and with my hand I gently ruffled Charlie's dirty blond hair.

'It's okay Charlie,' I said, over and over, but I knew it wasn't.

*

The following morning I phoned Shelly and she told me Charlie had spent a few hours in the hospital, but refused to stay any longer. His mother and father had declined to attend. He returned home against medical advice. The toxicology report confirmed Charlie had cocaine in his system. Charlie's social worker had been up-dated on the incident.

A week later in light of the incident the professionals gathered for a Specific Issues meeting. Ideas were bandied about and a strategy was decided upon. Under the circumstances it was thought some form of sanction should be put in place in an attempt to establish some sort of behaviour modification.

The staff at Acorn House should be congratulated, said the manager of the assessment team, not only in the way they had dealt with a potentially explosive situation, but in the way in which they had managed the overall level of risk to Charlie so far.

*

'I'm not going. They can fuck off,' Zoey shouted. She was stomping up and down the hallway knocking the framed pictures off the wall. A lamp came to rest at her feet and she kicked at it, breaking the shade. I had just walked through the front door for my late shift.

Little Sammy was in the lounge doorway with a drink in one hand and a bag of crisps in the other.

'What's happening', Zoey?' he asked calmly.

'They think they're moving me to Blackpool. No fuckin way.'

The day before Mavis had got the call from Zoey's social worker that an out of borough placement had been agreed and that the move was imminent. After Zoey had contracted anal gonorrhoea and been treated at the sexual health clinic, Social Services had finally decided to act. Mavis had slammed the phone down. 'The bitch wants me to break the news to the kid. She's not soft.'

By the looks of things Zoey hadn't taken the news well.

'Have you heard this, Jerry, they're moving me.'

'I haven't heard nothing,' I lied. 'I'm just going to get a handover.'

I stepped over the lamp and went in the office. Matt was counting the petty cash. He looked up.

'I figure Mavis told her then,' I said.

'Go 'way, how did you figure that?' said Matt grinning.

'I was joking.'

'I know.'

The office door opened and Mavis's head popped round. 'She wants to speak to her social worker.'

'Bring her in,' said Matt.

Zoey flopped into the chair while Matt punched the numbers and handed her the phone.

'Can I speak to Collette Davis?' asked Zoey.

Matt kept on counting. I put my coat in the cupboard and Mavis leaned against the radiator.

There was a knock on the door and little Sammy's face pressed at the glass. 'Can you get me a drink?'

'In a moment darling,' said Mavis.

Little Sammy kicked half-heartedly at the door and left.

'Well when will she be back?' said Zoey. She slammed the phone onto the desk. 'Bitch, she's gone home and isn't back in till Monday.'

'Friday, love,' said Mavis. 'They finish early on a Friday.'

'I don't give one, I'm not fuckin going,' said Zoey.

Matt closed the lid of the petty cash tin and placed it in the drawer. When he spoke his tone was gentle and sympathetic.

'What are you worried about?'

'I'm happy here,' said Zoey. The anger had gone out of her voice, replaced by sadness. 'I won't know anybody. Don't youse want me here?' she said, stung.

Matt came from behind the desk and perched himself in front of Zoey. 'Of course we want you, but you know that if you stay here it's not good for you mixing with people that are not right for you. Come on Zoey, in your heart you know I'm right.'

She looked up at Matt and gave a tentative nod.

'You'll soon make new friends,' added Mavis.

'Look on the bright side,' I said. You won't have to look at Matt's ugly face anymore.'

Zoey began to laugh.

'Good girl, you know it makes sense,' said Matt, 'you can phone us and maybe we can come and see you when you're settled in.'

She was smiling now.

'Why don't you let Mavis help you pack?' Matt went round the desk and took out the petty cash tin, 'I believe Carol has left you fifty quid to spend on a leaving present.'

Zoey left on the Sunday, Mavis took her. She phoned the first week she was there and said she was missing us all but soon enough the calls stopped. I guess by then she'd settled in. We did get the odd call from Blackpool saying Zoey was missing and to be on the lookout in case she made her way back to us. Eventually these stopped too.

***

Chapter 12

'Yer havin a fuckin giraffe aren't yer?' Charlie spat the words at Carol, the veins in his neck standing out like he was straining under a heavy weight. He was dressed in his usual afternoon attire, track suit bottoms and bare feet and chest. It had been decided at the Specific Issues meeting the week before, that due to Charlie's recent behaviours: the selling of his play station shortly after Christmas and the episode that saw him hospitalised due to his intake of cocaine and alcohol, his pocket money from now on would be spent with a member of staff.

'I'm sorry Charlie, but that's how it is until we see some marked improvement in your behaviour,' said Carol. Carol was team leader this particular Saturday due to Matt being off sick. I got the impression Carol was not too pleased at having to work the Saturday and the last thing she needed was Charlie kicking off.

‘Well I’ll just fuckin take the money,’ he said. He leaned over the desk and attempted to put his hand in the petty cash tin.

‘That’s up to you Charlie, but if you do then it will become a police matter,’ said Carol, firmly closing the lid of the tin.

‘Fuck you, get the fucking pigs, and see if I care. That’s all youse ever say, I’ll get the police and it will become a police matter,’ he ground the words out, nodding his head in short jerky movements, mocking Carol. Carol shot me a look and I knew it was time for me to step in, but I wasn’t sure any more where I stood with Charlie.

Before I could intervene Charlie picked up the large diary from the desk and sent it flying across the room. He then turned and half-wheeled half-threw a chair across the room. It crashed into the tin bin making more noise than it otherwise would have. He stood there, uncertain, before sitting on the floor.

‘I’m not leaving until I get my money.’

‘That’s up to you,’ said Carol, pretending to busy herself with the petty cash tin.

'Come on, Charlie, go and get dressed and I'll walk the shop with you and you can spend your money,' I said, trying to calm the situation. He ignored me and continued his rant at Carol,

'Just give me me money, yer grey-haired bitch before I punch yer fucking face in.'

If Carol was shaken by this she didn't let it show. She answered him calmly.

'Charlie, why don't you consider some drugs counselling? This isn't you. You were such a polite young boy when you came in.'

Charlie was sitting on the floor, his head in his hands. After making sure the petty cash tin was secure in the drawer, Carol walked round from behind her desk and continued, 'Why don't you have a talk with Jerry, you have a good relationship with him. I think you're feeling this way because it's the come down from the drugs you're using.'

'Fuck off yer grey-haired bitch.'

'Don't be like that. Carol's just trying to help you.'

'It's your choice Charlie, but if this behaviour continues then you're going to jeopardise your placement here,' said Carol.

Charlie numbly stared ahead, as if fixed on a thought, a memory. In his hand was a piece of *Blu Tac* that he was slowly rolling into balls with his index finger and thumb. A smile broke across his face and he started flicking the *Blu Tac* at Carol.

'Ay you, I wondered where all the *Blu Tac* was going,' said Carol.

Still smiling, he continued to flick the *Blu Tac* at her. He wasn't soft, he knew all Carol could do was request he stopped. Carol attempted to make light of it, but I could see Charlie was enjoying her discomfort.

'Come on you, behave yourself,' I said, reaching for the ball of *Blu Tac*. He looked at me and for a moment I thought he was about to say something, but he changed his mind and handed me the *Blu Tac*. He placed his hands on the desk and pulled himself up. Wiping his nose with the back of his hand he walked out the office.

I busied myself pretending to tidy the office desk, gathering up the loose *Blue Tac* until finally Carol, spoke.

'He's getting worse isn't he?'

'I know. I don't know what to say to him anymore. And the other week...he was... crazy.'

'It's because he's the big cheese in here now. If he continues on this path then he'll just end up in either a bed-and-breakfast or a hostel.'

'Can they do that?' I asked.

'Yes, of course they can. If he's not complying with the requirements of his care plan, then yes they can.' Carol raised her eyes towards the ceiling as if somewhere up above was the answer. 'What can you do?' she asked of no one in particular. 'He's not engaging on any level.' She looked at the calendar on the wall. The picture accompanying June showed a clear blue sky and a field full of poppies. A lone female figure walked amongst the flowers.

Someone had drawn a word balloon with the words *have a splif* coming from the woman's mouth.

'He's coming up to his sixteenth birthday soon and I'm afraid that changes everything.'

'In what way?' I said, but I already knew the answer. Matt had spoken about it on a number of occasions and Carol confirmed what I already knew.

'Charlie is only a section 20 and at sixteen if he's not going to engage with the service then they can discharge him. Do us a favour, Jerry, just go outside and keep an eye on them whilst I sort out the rest of the pocket money.'

Outside Charlie was on the front step smoking a cigarette with Eddy and little Sammy. I went through the motions and asked them to move off the step away from the building. They ignored me. Charlie was wrapped in a quilt, joking and laughing. He asked me if I would go the shop with him and buy him some bifftas. I explained, again for what felt like the millionth time, I couldn't do that as I would get the sack.

'I told yer Charlie lad, they're all the fucking same, just in it for the money,' snarled Eddy.

I wanted to challenge Eddy's viewpoint, but I knew from past experience it was a fruitless endeavour. I caught Charlie's eye and he flashed me a smile as if to say, same old Eddy. It was a nice gesture, but something had shifted in Charlie. A change, I sensed it. We both knew it but said nothing. We circled around it like a dead love affair. I hoped, deep down, Charlie understood and did know I cared. Whatever he thought, I had done the best I could.

*

Charlie became so cocooned in his drug stupor that money needed to be obtained on a daily basis. I reiterated to Charlie the risk he was running, that he would end up in a hostel but he was lost in the illusion that the Leaving Care Team would set him up in a flat.

It was here the first whisper of where Charlie's birth mother might be came to light. Matt told me that a new social worker, one not long out of University and, as he put it, 'With something to prove to the world,' was now in charge of Charlie's case and had been able (at Charlie's request) to trace the whereabouts of his birth mother.

This finding coincided with a further deterioration in Charlie's behaviour and in hindsight; it also served the interests of Social Services when it came to answering the question of what to do about Charlie.

I offered the usual incentives to get Charlie to curb his behaviour: mobile phone, football shirt and new trainers. Charlie failed to respond.

Any money he was allowed for travel to visit his family he would spend on cigarettes. This would then be recompensed out of his pocket money but even this proved pointless. What with his fines to pay to the courts and travel to pay back, Charlie amassed the debt of a small country. It was a fruitless endeavour. The Children's Act didn't make our job any easier as it stated a child had to be left with at least a third of its pocket money. This even applied when a kid smashed a piece of furniture or a television in anger.

Charlie, in desperate need of a constant supply of money, took little Sammy shoplifting. Exploitative behaviour whereby an older child pressured a younger child to become involved in illegal activity was taken quite seriously, not that little Sammy needed much persuasion. A Child in Public Care Meeting was called. The professionals took into consideration not only the risk Charlie was putting himself at, but also the level of risk posed to little Sammy (who was now thirteen) from Charlie.

The reviewing officer in a Child and Public Care Meeting has a lot more power and can take a case back to the Being Looked After Panel (BLA) if they believe it is the best way forward. This can result in the service to the child being withdrawn. It was at this point that the possibility of Charlie returning to his birth mother as soon as he was sixteen was mentioned and officially seen as a viable option.

When I learned of this I was happy for Charlie. I knew how important it was for him to one day find his birth mother and return to her and perhaps, I thought, this might go some way in helping to stabilise Charlie's behaviour and give him the sense of belonging he lacked. My joy soon turned to sadness.

'If you want my opinion, returning Charlie to his birth mother is simply the cheapest option for Social Services, said Matt. 'Over the years the lad's built up a romantic notion of his birth mother;

a kind of wounded angel, unable to cope with life and wanting the best for her kids.'

'Charlie might be right,' I challenged. 'Anyhow, who are we to judge?'

Matt scratched at his beard.

'Jerry, I've spoken to someone in the assessment team and according to them the mother's a pisshead and nothing like the wounded princess of Charlie's fairytale.'

It was decided before any contact took place, Charlie and his mother would communicate by letter and only then would the initial first contact be set up. Charlie also learned he had two step-brothers to add to his happy little family reunion.

Matt, through his contact in the assessment team, actually saw one of the letters the mother had sent to Charlie.

'It looks like it was written by a four-year-old,' said Matt.

'If that's the case then surely they won't allow Charlie to return to such an environment?.'

'He's sixteen, old enough to keep himself safe,' said Matt. 'Put it this way, it's either home with his mother or a hostel.'

Up until Charlie's discharge to the care of his birth mother Social Services were keeping him sweet. Charlie was given £240 pounds to spend with staff for his sixteenth birthday. 'One thing for sure,' said Matt. 'He'll be lucky if he gets a lollipop for his next birthday.'

*

Over the next few weeks I intentionally I tried to distance myself from Charlie. I took care of my keyworker duties, but beyond that I never got involved. I wasn't sure who I was trying to protect, me or Charlie. I don't know if Charlie was even aware of it, but it was there for all to see, if they cared to look.

When coming on shift Charlie would no longer be the kid I would seek out first and check how his weekend had been. I avoided being alone with him, fearing the approaching certainty of him leaving Acorn House.

My rhythm at home changed too. The tension was thick, as if I'd a dirty secret I was keeping from Kate. In a way it was a secret, a secret of shame and guilt for letting Charlie down.

'Want to talk about it?' said Kate.

I'd just settled Millie into bed, read her a story and the house was silent.

'It's Charlie isn't it?' said Kate.

The moment seemed right. 'I feel I've let him down, Kate. Perhaps if I'd taken him home to live with us like you said, things would be different.'

Kate moved her hair from the corner of her mouth. 'What will be, will be.'

'It's not just that.' I took a deep breath. 'I was thinking of asking Matt to swop me on the rota so I don't have to work on the day Charlie leaves. He need never know, but I just can't face being there when he goes. What a fucking coward I am.'

Kate's hand came to rest on mine. She snuggled closer, hugging me. The tension seeped out of me, melted into happier thoughts.

'Remember what you said to me?'

I hadn't a clue what she meant.

'You said you're not Jesus, and you were right. It's not your job to save him.'

***

Chapter 13

Charlie was carefully folding each item of clothing and placing it into an old battered army kit-bag. I sat on the edge of the bed watching him do this. Over in a corner, in a heap, were a number of muddy battered trainers and T-shirts, odd socks and torn track suit bottoms. Every so often Charlie stopped packing and discarded an item of clothing to the pile. I was about to interrupt the silence with a question when there was a tentative knock on the door. Mavis's head popped round. She was carrying a large sports bag, which she dropped to the floor.

'Hi Charlie, thought this might help. What you can't fit into that,' she said, nodding at the bag, 'we can always get your social worker to drop off in a few days when you're settled in.'

Charlie didn't acknowledge her and she shrugged her shoulders in a *please yourself* gesture and, after flashing me a smile, was gone.

Charlie moved across to the other side of the room and gently prised his Tupac poster from the wall. He carefully folded it, trying hard not to let it rip. He turned and shot me a grin at the hole now visible in the wall. The hole caused by me all those months before. We both laughed.

'That was laughin',' he said, recalling the memory, 'When me and Eddy were smoking in here.'

'Oh that reminds me,' I said, and reaching into my jacket pocket I threw him 40 cigarettes.

'Now don't say a fucking thing or you'll get me shot.'

'Nice one, Jerry lad.' He placed the cigarettes in his bag, laughing to himself and I knew he was thinking about all the times I'd gone on about smoking being bad for him.

'I wasn't here for your birthday last week and it's…it's a goodbye gift too.' I really didn't know what else to get him, what else he would appreciate. I felt the card inside my inner pocket bend as he gave me a hug. 'Oh, there's something else, I said. 'I know staff all signed a goodbye card for you, but I wanted to get you one myself.' I handed him the bent card.

He ripped the envelope open and read the card to himself. A smile broke across his face.

'Nice one,' he said.

I wanted to write something profound, but in the end simply wrote:

The best of luck, take care,
Jerry.

I sat back with my hands behind my head trying to look relaxed before I asked the question that was on my mind.

'So, how did the meeting with your mum go?' I hated to ask this. Matt had already told me the feeling from the social worker was Charlie had been rather disappointed in what he saw, but had maintained a brave face when the individual presented to him as his birth mother didn't match the flawless work of art he'd created in his head for all those years.

'Good,' he said, stuffing clothes into the bag.

'Yeah well give us a little bit more, was it…you know…' I searched around for the right words, 'I mean was it *difficult?* Did it go okay?'

'Yeah, good,' he said, nodding his head before adding, 'I think it was difficult for both of us. I'm looking forward to meeting my step-brothers.'

'Good, good,' I said. 'So, I hear the plan is for you to be discharged Friday?'

Charlie nodded. He looked up before throwing an old sock into the pile.

'Are you in work Friday?'

'No. I'm not down to work.' The words felt empty, like someone else had said them. Kate was right; I wasn't Jesus. At that moment I felt more like Judas.

Charlie smiled and patted my arm. 'No worries, Jerry lad, catch you next time.'

For all his confidence he seemed unsure and I thought to myself: *fuck who wouldn't be? It's only natural.* We talked some more, small talk, about the football on Saturday until finally, there was nothing left to say.

'Yeah well, I hope it all works out for you.'

'Cheers, Jerry lad,' he said with a grin.

I stood and we hugged.

'Take care, kid.' I turned to leave. 'Charlie?'

He looked up from his kit-bag but I couldn't look him in the eyes. I half-closed the door so it hid my face. I could feel my eyes beginning to water.

'Stay out of trouble and keep off all the shit,' my voice trailed off. I took a deep breath before adding, 'take care, kid.'

That was the last time I saw Charlie. The circle was complete. The very mother he was removed from for his own protection, he was now reunited with.

*

Six months later Charlie's social worker was doing a statutory visit at the home and I asked her if she knew how Charlie was getting on. She told me that she was no longer his social worker. The last she'd heard Charlie was serving two years in a young offender's institution for possession of class A drugs with intent to supply.

'I'm sorry,' she said. 'I know you were close.'

The good news was, whilst in prison, Charlie accessed the drug programme. Her information was sketchy but it seemed Charlie became involved with one of his newly discovered cousins, Dean, a well-schooled criminal. It was sad news and I received it with a heavy heart, but to say I was shocked would be a lie. Matt had prepared me for it. I could see Matt now, his arms spread wide like a picture of Jesus welcoming all sinners proclaiming:

'This is as good as it gets my son. Jerry, it's out of your hands, you did your best. You're forgiven for thinking you could change shit. Now, go forward and sin no more my son.'

***

There was no one to cover the shift and Carol asked me if I was up for a try at shift leading, all the responsibilities of a team leader but without the higher rate of pay and although I felt nervous at the prospect, I was also invigorated and thrilled to be asked.

Four days earlier there had been a new admission. A 14-year-old girl named, Chloe. Her mother and step-father couldn't control her, she'd run away from home on a number of occasions but always turned up at her boyfriend's flat, a 23-year-old. She'd been at another children's home but had beaten a girl up and was sent to us for respite. We all knew this was no temporary fixture. She would be staying, long- term.

Chloe was a wiry young thing, mousey hair, blue eye shadow and tonnes of mascara gave her panda eyes. She looked no more than twelve, but was attempting to look older.

So there I was, playing team leader, me and Debbie, the night staff. 10:45pm and we were trying to settle the kids for bed. To be honest, up to this point the kids hadn't been too much trouble;

apart from little Sammy smoking in his bedroom, things had run smoothly.

'Come on you lot, in your rooms, time for bed, let's get you settled now,' I said.

The door to Chloe's room was open and Bethany and little Sammy were sitting on the end of her bed. Eddy was on the floor, his back against the wall.

'Oh chillax,' said Chloe, turning up the music.

Eddy let out a squeal of a laugh. Since Chloe's arrival he'd been like a dog with two dicks. I surveyed the room and I knew I would have to stamp my authority right off or it was going to be a long night. I ran through the familiar steps:

'Come on children, bedtime. If anyone wants supper best head to your rooms.' There was no immediate move and I was about to repeat myself when Debbie's voice cut in.

'Come on, Chloe, honey, what would you like for your supper?'

I knew what Debbie was doing, working on the premise that if she could settle Chloe with the promise of supper the rest of the kids would follow suit.

'A big fat cock,' said Chloe.

The children laughed, sniggered at our discomfort, but Debbie was not impressed. Her face became serious and she stepped towards Chloe. It was unexpected and for a brief moment Chloe seemed unsure, but any uncertainty that Chloe may have held was gone in a flicker.

'How dare you talk like that to me, you a young girl. You show some respect when you talk to me.'

The children laughed.

'What's a matter, have you never had a big fat fucking cock?' said Chloe, turning away, reaching over and increasing the volume on her music.

'Look,' I said, raising my voice, 'get to your rooms otherwise I'll call the police and have you all done for breach of the peace.' I had witnessed Shelly use the same tactic once, successfully, albeit at two o' clock in the morning.

'Wah? Are you havin' a laugh?' Chloe shouted at me. She glared at me trying to figure out if I was bluffing and then she looked to the other kids. Bethany drifted off to her room with the promise of toast and orange juice.

'Come on love,' said Debbie to little Sammy, 'if you want your football shirt tomorrow you'd better move it.'

Little Sammy had been promised if he was good and settled at bedtime he could spend his savings with his keyworker in the morning. The promise of a new football shirt won him over. Eddy was not so co-operative and did what he had to do to save face in front of Chloe. He raised himself up in front of me and said to Chloe, 'Fancy a biffta?'

'Alright,' said Chloe with a grin. They left the room, sliding past us.

*

The next day I was in the office, five minutes before handover, when the doorbell rang I could see through the glass, a young lad standing on the step, shaven head, a scar above his right eye that had scabbed but still looked sore. He was wearing a black tracksuit and a Man United football shirt. I opened the door. He wet his finger and thumb and nipped the end of his cigarette out. He spat on the step before he spoke.

'Are you Jerry?'

'Yeah, I'm Jerry.

'I'm Owen.' The name seemed familiar but I couldn't place the lad's face. 'Chloe's boyfriend,' he added.

'Oh yes, I said,' a little surprised. We'd been told not to encourage Chloe's relationship with the lad due to the age gap and the negative influence Chloe's family said he was having on her. Plus she was underage. Fucking pervert, I thought. It still never struck me how he knew my name.

'What can I do you for?' I asked.

'Can I have a word?'

'Yeah sure. What's the problem?'

'Chloe says that last night you told her she had a nice arse and that you're always looking at her funny.'

I stepped back unsure of what I'd just heard. My hand came up and I rubbed the night's growth of bristles on my chin. With sleeping in I'd not showered or shaved. I felt sticky, my clothes felt grubby. The gentle rhythms of a headache I'd had all morning, due to lack of sleep, suddenly became an intense rush. I looked at him searching for a trace of fun in his eyes, the punch line but his eyes were hard, bright and serious. I gathered myself.

'Do me a favour mate, just wait here and I'll be back in a minute.'

I closed the door and left him on the step. I returned with Matt and asked the lad to repeat what he'd said with Matt as a witness.

I was sent home and told to wait for a phone call. I was terrified. Kate was chopping salad when I arrived home. Millie was over at her grandmother's. Apart from the low murmur of the radio the house was at peace. I told Kate about the day's events. We sat in silence, stunned.

*

It took three long hours before the recourse manager, Victoria Gray contacted me. She asked if I had any annual leave left. A few days I said.

'I think,' she said, her words emotionless, 'you should take a few days leave until matters are resolved.'

Until matters are resolved, the words echoed like a death sentence. For some reason I thought she was phoning to see if I was okay, but it struck me it was the girl she was concerned about. It rapidly became clear there was nowhere to move the child so I couldn't return to work.

'No,' I said firmly. 'I won't take annual leave because I've done nothing wrong. Am I suspended?'

'No, of course not, but you will have to take a few days off whilst we investigate this incident. She paused. 'With pay, of course.'

'Incident,' I said. 'What incident? Nothing happened, the girl's lying.' She paused again. 'We have to think of the child.'

'What about me?'

The air crystallised, the moment and the gravity of the situation suddenly became clearer. 'Are you saying you believe her?' I said my voice tight.

'No, I'm saying we have to investigate. Jerry, calm yourself, all jobs have their risk and allegations are just part and parcel of the job. From time to time they happen.'

You patronising cunt. The words stopped, caught in my throat, self- preservation kicking in before they could escape.

'Yeah, but if I was a fireman and I got killed rescuing a child from a burning building I would be a hero. That kind of risk I can live with but this…this just leaves me cold.'

She didn't even try to rebuke my argument. She knew I was right but she didn't care. What was it to her? I was expendable.

'I can hear you're a little upset. Try and relax and I'll contact you shortly. Goodbye, Jerry.'

*

The allegation was like a black hole, with me at its centre. No light could enter without being swallowed up in a pool of depression. You fall deeper, deeper than loneliness, until you're fully enveloped by blackness.

I didn't sleep. My days were heavy even when Millie skipped into the room, her features soft and glowing with happiness. She knew something was wrong with Daddy; had heard Daddy and Mummy shouting at each other, but she didn't ask.

I couldn't tell anyone, I *dared* not tell anyone outside of Kate. What if word got out and people thought it was true?

Matt phoned and told me not to worry.

'Everyone knows she's a lying little fucker.'

Finally, a week later the call came. I was to meet with a Mr. Williams while he questioned me about the incident. Only weeks before, I'd dithered about joining the union. Matt had recently become our new union rep and it was only at his persuasion I'd taken up the offer.

*

Matt and I were left waiting for fifteen minutes before handshakes and introductions at nine-fifteen.

Mr. Williams indicated for us to be seated. His grey hair was slicked back. He was clean-shaven with red cheeks. His suit looked crisp, fresh as if it had been purchased that morning.

'How are you Jerry?' His voice was pleasant, chatty and he immediately put me at ease.

'Not good.'

'Okay,' he said, giving me a sympathetic smile. 'As you know this is just an informal chat so please feel free, at any point, to ask any questions you may have.'

I nodded.

'If you don't mind I'm going to take a few notes just for my own records.' He took out a slim black Parker pen from his inside pocket and moved his chair forward.

Matt followed suit, flicking the top of his biro.

'Perhaps you would be kind enough to describe what took place regarding the said incident,' asked Mr. Williams.

I gave my account and after it was over there was silence. A telephone rang somewhere outside. He studied me for a moment. I met his gaze. Did I look guilty to him? I couldn't read anything in his clear green eyes. Matt shifted on his chair and straightened a crease in his trousers, ran his thumb up and down the seam. His usual white trainers had been replaced by shiny black shoes.

‘Why do you think the child would say,’ Mr. Williams looked at the paper in front of him, ‘you told her she had a nice arse?’

I let out a long breath. ‘I never said that.’ His eyes betrayed no flicker of whether he believed me or not. I continued, ‘I’ve no idea. Perhaps she just doesn’t like me.’

‘Had anything happened to make you think that?’ he said, gently probing. I could feel myself growing tense, angry at being subjected to this.

‘I think I upset her.’

He nodded.

I went on. ‘A day or two before she’d come down the stairs as I was tidying up after supper, all dolled up with one of the other kids, Bethany, and asked me how old I thought she looked. I told her about twelve. I told her if she went out she’d be reported missing from care. She told me to fuck off.’

The rage had been pent up too long, over too many sleepless nights of worry, of hushed tones in bed with Kate. I looked to Matt, a side glance, he sensed nothing, but Williams did. He picked up on the electric charge of energy in the air. I could see it in his eyes the way his gaze wavered, and in the way he hesitantly fingered the knot in his tie.

'Look, let's get this straight. There's nothing that I would ever find sexually attractive about a 14-year-old child. Not in this life or any other.' I felt my eyes start to fill with tears of rage. I couldn't stop now even if I wanted to.

'For fuck's sake, I have a young daughter.'

Matt's hand was on my shoulder, a calming touch, but it was too late. Tears were on my cheeks and I fumbled for a piece of tissue. I had to blow my nose before we could continue.

'Would you like to take a few moments, Jerry? It's not my intention to upset you.'

I fixed him with a stare. He remained as still as a photograph. 'With all due respect Mr. Williams, what did you expect, party streamers?'

'Obviously,' said Matt, taking over, his voice calm and in control. 'It's plain to see what's happened here. This girl, unable to get her own way, has taken a dislike to Jerry and made all this up to get back at him.'

'Yeah, it had to be me. It would hardly have had the same impact if she'd said it about Debbie,' I said.

A confused look crossed Mr. Williams' face. 'I'm sorry, but who's Debbie?'

I looked across to Matt and saw the disbelief registered on his face.

'Debbie. Debbie is the night care worker at Acorn House who was with me all the time. She never left my side.'

A vacant look shot across Mr. Williams' face like someone on the end of a private joke.

'I see,' he said.

'Have you not spoken with the night staff?' I asked.

His smooth fingers lightly fingered his tie, the colour dropping from his cheeks.

'I'm afraid I was unaware that—'

'Well, before we go any further I suggest you fucking talk to her,' I barked.

Matt's hand gently touched my shoulder, hushing me before I went any further.

*

The call came the next day. Debbie confirmed my story and no formal investigation was necessary. I could return to work. I didn't want to but I had bills and a mortgage to pay. I thought about leaving, I really did, weighed it up, as carefully as one weighs gold but there were no jobs at least not any that provided regular hours. I would go forward but from now on I would practise what Matt preached.

When I did return to work I was a shadow of myself. Afraid in case the girl made something else up. It was all too much and I ended up going off sick for a month with stress.

Shortly afterwards Chloe was moved to another home for an assault on Bethany. Two weeks after that she made an allegation against another member of staff. She played the same tactic word for word.

A poor damaged child inflicting damage on others, said Carol.

***

Part Two

Melissa's Story

Rather lead and be mistaken than
Following and fakin for the
Sake of seeming true.
(Roddy Frame)

But they say it's a swell joint no
School…no cops
You can tear the place apart
And nobody sez a word…
Loaf around, plenty to
Eat, plenty to drink and
It's all free. Boy that's the place.
(Lampwick, talking to Pinocchio about Pleasure Island)

Chapter 14

One year later:

Five minutes and I'll be ready.

Five minutes.

Just five minutes…

'Mirror, mirror on the wall why the fuck am I still doing this?' I asked myself this every early shift.

'Money boy, money,' was my only answer.

I cupped the water in my hands and swilled it over my face. I swallowed and my throat hurt on one side. I'd had a sore throat for about two weeks now. I'd thought about seeing a doctor but I knew she'd just say it was a virus and it would clear on its own. I rubbed my hand over my face; I needed a shave, but it could wait another day. It's not like I was off to visit the Queen.

I looked in on Millie. She was sleeping, lost in her dreams. It was six o' clock and she wasn't up for school for another two hours. I padded quietly to the bedroom and felt about for my car keys on the dresser. Kate was pretending to be asleep. I played along.

***

Chapter 15

I arrived for my late shift fifteen minutes late. The handover was already underway and I apologised and blamed it on the traffic. The handover consisted of the usual stuff: No kids went to school or to their alternative educational placement. One of the children was bringing pot into the building, and there was no team leader cover for the following night. There was a note in my tray:

Jerry, you're now to keywork Melissa, as Mavis is not returning to work. Let Laura Roberts, Melissa's social worker, know you're now the keyworker. For background information

READ THE FILE!!!

Carol.

I knew a little about Melissa and had spoken with her on occasion. She was a thirteen-year-old section 31. She'd been at Acorn House for three months. Her keyworker had been Mavis until she'd been assaulted by Leon, a violent 14-year-old twat currently placed at Acorn House. Mavis had been on long term sick since the assault and decided it was time to move on.

Melissa was louder than she looked. Not so much petite looking, more undernourished. Skinny sickly would perhaps best describe her physical frame. Her face was pinched, pale, and anxious, framed by long black hair. I showed Matt the note.

'Fuck me, Jerry, you better dig your gas mask out,' he said, laughing.

For the last two months Melissa had begun to stink. It was a foul smell that was growing stronger. No one seemed too concerned, putting it down to the kid not washing.

'Cheers Matt.' I thumbed thorough Melissa's file looking for the social worker's number. 'Why me man? I think she'd be better off with a female worker.' From the little I did know, Melissa was hard work.

'It's all experience, Jerry.'

'It's just more shit and you know it.'

'Well you better get used to shit because she stinks of it.'

I was too pissed off to laugh. I phoned Laura Roberts. It took a few minutes for her to come to the phone. I told her that I was taking over from Mavis; she didn't even ask why Mavis had left.

'Melissa is the product of a foster breakdown. There's also a nine-year-old stepsister, Lizzy. Lizzy is black and still with the foster family.'

'Why were they split?' I asked.

'Melissa was with them for nine months before her behaviour became problematic. She'd go missing for days on end usually ending up back at her mother's house. It's not that she can't see her mum but contact must be supervised.'

I looked over at Matt and rolled my eyes. 'Why were they removed in the first place?'

Laura Robert's voice became muffled as she placed her hand over the receiver and said something in answer to a voice in the background. 'Neglect, the mother's an alcoholic and a prostitute. She frequently left the children outside her local pub or at home alone often with no food. She also admitted to hitting the children. Following an investigation Social Services applied for a full care order on both children.' Her voice took on a thin edge of disgust. 'We also suspect that Melissa may have witnessed her mother having sex with a variety of men for money. Melissa herself has a poor self-image, low self-esteem. There's no evidence but I believe she may have been sexually abused by more than one of the mother's frequent paying partners.'

I wasn't shocked. One thing I'd learned; the world was full of scum- bags.

'What about the fathers?' I asked.

'The whereabouts of both are unknown.'

'Is the mother in a relationship at the moment?'

'Yes, we think so but she tells us very little.'

I let out a long whistle. 'I can see why we need supervised contact.'

The phone went dead for a moment.

'Look, all of this should be in the file,' she said, impatiently.

'Okay, one last thing. Are you aware of Melisa's odour problem?' I looked over at Matt who was holding his nose, his cheeks puffed out. 'Could she have a phobia about washing?'

'Not to my knowledge. Mavis had mentioned something a few weeks ago and something about abdominal pains. I don't know if the two were related but I did notice the smell when I last visited. As far as I know a doctor's appointment had been made and Melissa gave a urine sample.'

'What were the results?'

'Again, as far as I'm aware the results were negative. Her voice was rushed and I could tell she just wanted to get off the phone. 'No infection was evident.' She paused. 'If the odour is still persisting, then it may be just as well to get her checked again just in case there is a link with the tummy pain.'

'I agree.'

'Okay, I really have to go, busy day today, just read the file.'

'Okay, Laura I'll be in touch, bye.'

She was gone. For a moment I stood rubbing the tiredness out of my eyes. Keeping the girl safe was going to be difficult. I would have to make sure I logged and recorded everything. I'd only been in one hour and already I felt like a pressure cooker.

*

It was Wednesday late shift before I got to have a chat with Melissa about being her new keyworker. James was the team leader. I entered the office and reached for the signing in sheet. I was late again. There was a space on the sheet requesting the reason. I drew a line and took off my coat.

'Leave your coat on, Jerry, you have to go straight back out,' said James. 'Your great skills are needed.'

There was no sarcasm intended, James liked to be optimistic. His manner was brighter than usual today and his cheerfulness blinded me more than usual. A nice bloke, I liked him. He'd had polio as a child and it left him with a limp in his left leg. It got worse when he was tired but for James the glass was always half-full. In the short time he'd been at Acorn House the worst I heard him say was *'damm'.* James had become as much a part of Acorn House as the cigarette stumps on the front step. He never seemed to go home. If a shift needed covering James was there. He called it a *'collective responsibility.'* I called it foolish.

'What toilet do you need cleaning James?'

He smiled handing me the minibus keys. 'It's Melissa. She's been caught shoplifting in *Glitzy Bits.* The police need an appropriate adult to attend at the station whilst they do the interview. The duty solicitor is on his way so you shouldn't be too long.'

'Great, more fucking paper work.'

'Remember, Jerry, all behaviour is communication.'

'Oh come on she gets ten quid pocket money a week why does she have to shoplift?' I thought for a moment and then answered my own question. 'Maybe she's communicating the money's not enough.'

'She's a very troubled girl.'

'Okay, climb down off your social work hand book, I'm going.'

A look of pain crossed over James's face as he went into a fit of coughing.

'You okay?' I asked.

'Yes. Just a bad chest that's all.'

'Those ciggies they'll kill you in the end.'

'Jerry, it's me only pleasure,' he coughed.

*

I entered the police station through the side entrance. The waiting room was deserted apart from an old man slumped on a chair reading a newspaper. I pushed the buzzer to let them know I was there. After a few moments I heard the door being unlocked and a female police officer in her early twenties ushered me in.

'This way please.'

'Another one of yours Jerry,' said the desk sergeant with a smile.

I glanced up and saw myself on the CCTV monitor. I looked old and tired. Behind the sergeant's desk was a small alcove of a room and the sound of a television was just audible.

'Yeah, we should get commission the number of kids we send through here.'

The sergeant laughed and turned to the woman officer who had shown me in. 'Sally, will you let them know Jerry's here?'

She nodded and strode down the corridor.

'Take a seat, they'll call when ready.'

I sat down wishing I'd brought a newspaper or a book. The clock on the wall showed 3:15 pm. I checked my watch and it was near enough the same, give or take a minute. Great, another eight hours before my shift was over. I was lost in thought when a police officer came out of one of the far interview rooms, a tall imposing man with an intimidating stare. I hadn't seen this officer before and figured he must be new.

'This way please.'

As we walked down the corridor I made a tentative effort at conversation. 'Has she behaved herself?' I didn't really give a fuck, but I played the professional.

'Yes. No trouble, but all the same we're glad you're here, as the smell from her is disgusting.'

At first I was a little taken aback by his forwardness, but I guessed he was a straight-to-the-point person. 'Yeah, I know, we're trying to find out what's causing it.'

We entered a room a little bigger than a walk-in cupboard. No natural light just a single fluorescent tube reflecting off the apple-white walls. Straightaway the smell hit me. It was as if someone had taken a shit in the corner of the room. There was a small table and four chairs off to one side. The tall police man closed the door behind me and indicated for me to take a seat.

Over to my right was a man in a suit that had an air of expense and class about it, unlike its occupant. This was Charlie O' Brian, one of the regular duty solicitors. I wondered what he saw when he was faced with *another* kid in care in the police station. Fucking pound signs, that's what. God, I doubted the parasite ever got tired of earning money.

He flashed me a smile revealing blinding white teeth. He was in mid- flow. 'I tell you what, P.C Hallcroft, United were extremely lucky with that penalty on Saturday.'

'When you're a winner good fortune tends to go your way,' replied Hallcroft.

'I wouldn't know I'm an Everton fan,' said O Brian.

We all laughed. I wasn't really interested I was just being polite.

'How's PC Martin?' asked O Brian, to the tall officer that had let me in. 'Did she have the baby?'

'Yes. A baby girl, named Lisa. Seven pound six ounces, she's sent a picture in. Stick around later and I'll show it to you.'

Throughout all this Melissa was sitting to the left smiling, chin in her hands, elbows on the table.

'Hi Jerry, Jerry, Jerry,' she sung. 'Where's Tom?'

I forced a smile. 'Yeah, very funny, Tom's out shoplifting,' I answered sarcastically. 'Tom and Jerry,' I said, explaining the joke to the tall police officer behind me.

'Okay,' said officer Hallcroft clapping his hands together, 'let's do this interview.'

*

'Get your seat belt on, Melissa or you're walking,' I said.

'Mel, I don't like Melissa,' she said, in a tiny mock five-year-old voice.

'Whatever, *Mel,* get your seat belt on.'

'Can we stop? I need a fucking biffta.'

'No we have to get back,' I said, starting the minibus.

'Oh you're a meany,' she said in a tiny voice.

'Yeah well, this meany's going to be your new keyworker.'

There was no reaction to this, no waving of arms, no facial expression and no vocal protest, tiny or otherwise. We stopped at the lights and I opened the window on my side.

'Jerry, it's freezing.'

'Yeah well, I get hot.' I lied. The odour coming from Mel was making me sick. She must have been aware of it. How could she not have been? It smelt like a dead animal.

When I was a kid I came across a dead cat. It must have been in the bushes for weeks. It was sprawled on its side and the smell coming from it stung my nostrils, assaulted my senses. The maggots had eaten away most of its eye and it was hard to make out its tortoise-shell pattern because the maggots had swarmed into a mass of living larvae and slowly, instinctively, relentlessly they were working their way over the cat's carcass. I'd felt a sting of pity for the animal and was unable to shake the memory of the stench of rotten flesh for days. Mel brought it all back. For a while we drove in silence.

'Is Mavis coming back?'

I shook my head and quickly drove around a bus that had pulled into a bus stop.

'Is it because Leon twatted her?'

'I don't know. Anyway, you need to stop shoplifting,' I said not wanting to discuss poor Mavis or that little bastard Leon. 'They've charged you this time.'

'I don't care.'

'You will if you get locked up.' As soon as I'd said it I regretted it. Mel knew and I knew that it would never happen, but by now such talk, on my part, was just a reflex.

'Look,' Mel shouted, pointing out the window at the grass verge, 'bunnies.'

Apart from me refusing to put on a CD, the type of shit music that sounds like someone's building a shed, played so loud the speakers distort, the drive back to the home was uneventful.

*

'I see you like pink,' I said, letting Mel into her bedroom.

Half-empty yogurt pots and cups littered the windowledge. In the far corner was a pink canvas wardrobe but from the look of the clothing covering the floor I wondered why Mel needed a wardrobe. Next to it was a pink TV sitting on top of a pink DVD player. The TV was still on and must have been left on all night. A grey, unmade, metal framed bed was situated under the window, framed by pink curtains. On the bed was a pink heart-shaped pillow with the word *Mother* embroidered at its centre.

A Winnie-the-Pooh lamp sat on a bedside table also left on, its shade smeared with chocolate finger prints. A matching rug was slung on the floor, Winnie-the-Pooh's face peeked out through the clothes that covered it.

Open compacts of make-up littered the bedroom floor, assorted shoes and boots were scattered along with plastic shopping bags. A lone black bin bag filled with clothes stood slumped and exhausted in one corner, while at its base rested a hairdryer and hair straighteners side by side, their wires curled and intertwined. The whole room gave off the stench of musky unwashed clothes.

The back of the door was covered in felt-tip writing: *Smoke weed, get stoned, JEZ WUZ ERE,* the usual montage of creativity and the walls were a collage of, what I assumed to be, Mel's mother and extended family. Pictures that showed Mel younger: as a baby, as a four-year-old sitting next to a young mum on a brown sofa.

'Why don't you get yourself a nice bubble bath before tea?' I said.

'Bye, bye,' said Mel, mimicking a five-year-old's voice before slamming the door in my face.

***

Chapter 16

'FOD!' The open palm of Leon's hand slapped against my forehead. I had literally just walked through the door. Violence takes many forms in residential care: the verbal assault can hurt your heart, but the physical enrages me.

FOD was Leon's new game; his new method of attack. It's only a *game*, but like the persistent jab of a well-schooled boxer it took its toll on the opponent.

'Alright, Leon cut it out.'

'Alright, Jerry chill, it's just a joke.'

'You're the joke lad. How many times have we been through this? This is my personal space,' I said drawing an imaginary line between us, 'and this is your space,' I pointed to Leon's side of the imaginary line.

Leon was a 14-year-old shaven redhead, smelling of Lynx deodorant. It barely masked the smell of stale sweat. All the stereotypical features of the anti-social youth converged in one place; freckled faced with two large front teeth squashed into a tiny mouth. Eyes as green as emeralds. Eyes that never trust.

'Are you going into the office?'

'Yes,' I answered, 'why?'

Leon sniffed. ''Cos ask can I have my travel money now? I've been waiting all fuckin day.'

'Should you not be in school?'

Leon looked at me as if I'd just spoken Russian.

'I don't do school,' replied Leon.

I let out a small laugh. 'What you mean Leon is that you choose not to do school.' I shook my head in despair. 'Tell me Leon, have you ever seen the movie Pinocchio?'

A puzzled look crossed over Leon's face. 'Wah?'

'Well you should,' I said, 'especially the bit where Pinocchio goes off to Pleasure Island.'

He didn't get the reference and I couldn't be arsed explaining it to him.

It was a day or two before when Matt had come up with the best analogy of the care system yet. He'd been watching Pinocchio with his young grandchild when the vision came to him.

'Jerry, I tell yer, care is just like that bit in Pinocchio where the kids go off to Pleasure Island. They smoke, drink, don't go to school and smash things up to their hearts' content. Slowly they all turn into donkeys; first the ears then the tails until, fuck me they're a fucking donkey working down the mines. That's what we do Jerry, we produce fucking donkeys.'

I turned and put my key in the office door. Leon slapped the back of my head and punched me in the back, hard enough to hurt and a sharp pain shot up my left kidney. Five minutes I'd been in and already I wanted to drop the little ginger cunt. I turned to face him and he slapped me '*playfully*' on the top of my head. I put my hand up to fend off the slap and this just made him want to try harder. I pushed him back on the shoulder with the palm of my hand sending him backwards off balance.

'Cut it out, Leon.'

He paid me no heed and came forward grinning, his two front teeth rejoicing in the space the grin allowed them. This time I took my left hand and made a fist; placing a half protruding finger in to Leon's solar- plexus I pushed. This was not an agreed physical response in line with THINK FIRST training, but I did it anyway.

Leon went off like a Catherine wheel.

'Hey, who yer pushin?'

The pain etched over his face; his two front teeth retreated. I felt a deep satisfaction.

'Personal space Leon, remember.' I spat the words.

'Do ya wanna fight?' His face was now as red as his hair and there's nothing I would have liked better than to drop him; shut him up. I bet then he would never tell me to fuck off again or FOD me. But of course I didn't, I had to take his shit and eat it,put my dignity in my back pocket and not take it out until my shift was over. Over time I had learned this, but it wasn't easy.

'Go for it Leon,' I said calmly, 'and I'll have you arrested for assault.'

'Fuck off.' Leon vomited the words but gave no ground. I, on the other hand, knew the score; you always had to give them a way out; a way of not losing face. The buzz of the doorbell broke the moment. It was Terry, one of the kids.

'Where's he been?' I asked, taking the opportunity to break the tension, water it down.

'Shaggin yer wife,' said Leon, running to open the door. I let out a long sigh; a sigh of resignation for the shift to follow.

'Got any bifftas?' I heard Leon ask Terry. I opened the office door and retreated.

*

I was greeted almost simultaneously by Shelly and Margaret.

'Hi lovely, how are you?' asked Shelly.

I unzipped my coat and placed it over the back of a chair. Off to one side there was a stack of what looked like newly wrapped curtains and such.

'I'm good thanks, Shelly, what's with all the stuff?' I asked, nodding towards the flowered materials.

'New bedding for the kids' rooms, Carol's allocated them fifty pounds each to do up their rooms, in conjunction with their keyworkers of course.'

I couldn't help but smile. 'Is there an inspection due?' I asked.

Now an even bigger smile broke across Shelly's face, 'Now, now, Jerry, one must not be cynical,' said Shelly with a wagging finger.

'It's the rebel in me, Shell.'

'The 17th,' said Shelly, laughing.

I walked over and checked my tray to see what wonderful delights and news had been added to my day. There was a note from Carol telling me she had changed my day shift on Wednesday to a late. 'Great, a fucking late,' I said.

Shelly shot me a look of sympathy. 'I know lovely, but Lucy has phoned in sick so she had to take you off your day shift and put you on the late.'

'What's up with her?' Lucy was new. She'd only been with us a month. I guess she was about 26 or 27, not much older, very bubbly and always smiling.

'Diarrhoea.'

I laughed. This was the usual thing staff phoned in with if they wanted a few days off.

'Who was that coming in, Jerry?' asked Margaret her head in a file. She was shortly going off shift and was fully absorbed in the writing of that morning's client diaries. Terry coming in would mean she'd have to go back on herself and log the time he'd returned.

'Just Terry, Leon's in the building too.'

'He's been a right little bastard, he was on the roof last night, couldn't get him out of the office before,' said Shelly.

'Threatened to punch me because he wasn't allowed travel money,' added Margaret.

'You've always got your THINK FIRST, training,' I said with a smile. 'Pity it didn't work for poor Mavis.'

They both laughed but,it was a forced laughter. It lit up an uncomfortable memory for them. It brought all *our* guilt to the surface. I could see it etched on their faces, my own cowardice included.

*

I'd been in the kitchen tidying up after tea when I heard the scream. By the time I got there it was all but over. Mavis was slumped in a chair in the main office, tears rolling down her face, great sobs coming from her. Her head hung like a wounded bird, her forehead wrinkled with lines of pain and beads of perspiration had gathered, multiplying like cells. James, the team leader, was standing over her.

'Easy now, Mavis, the ambulance is on its way,' said James. 'Try to stay calm, take deep breaths.'

Mavis was holding on to James's hand whilst her other lay limp, its weight dragging her down, causing her pain. Her shoulder had been dislocated by the force of the office door crashing into her, Leon helping it on its way. Leon had wanted to use the phone, but in the past when given the phone Leon had walked off refusing to give it back; chasing up his drugs for the weekend.

In an effort to stop him ordering his drugs Carol said whenever Leon needed to used the phone it must be supervised by staff and only in the office. Mavis had simply followed orders and Leon, as Mavis was closing the office door had pushed with all his hate knocking Mavis over. She'd landed awkwardly and her shoulder had popped out like a new born baby.

'Where's Leon now?' I asked.

'Done a runner,' answered James.

'Shall I get the police?' I asked.

James lowered his eyes. 'I don't know.'

'James, it's assault, he did it on purpose,' I said.

'Get the police. I want the little bastard done.' Mavis's voice cut in, desperate and hurt, her eyes pleading and the decision was made.

Leon was arrested. Incident forms were hastily filled in. A Specific Issues Meeting was called. Leon admitted assault and was given a referral order for nine months. Higher management were not happy that Mavis had pressed charges and in their words, 'criminalised the child.'

Mavis went off sick with stress and was offered a move to another home. She fought back and asked the council why she should be the one to be moved? She'd done nothing wrong, but it seemed it wouldn't be in Leon's best interests to move him. But we were all guilty. We all threw the letters from Mavis's solicitor in the bin requesting a statement regarding our working practices and conditions. Carol took us one by one into her office and told us we were free to do what we wanted but if we supported Mavis's claim, it may not be looked on favourably by the council. We all scattered like rabbits afraid for our mortgages.

*

'Yeah, he's got great potential that Leon. I tell you it's only a matter of time before he does another one of us. He should have been moved.' I went over to the door and looked through the glass to make sure Leon wasn't ear-wigging. 'He must think he walks on fucking water,' I said.

Already I was tense. I could feel it creeping up into my shoulders, stalking me like a bad prophecy. I felt smaller, reduced physically and spiritually by the thought of the shift ahead of me. Not all the kids used physical violence, but the threat was always there, the anarchy of the whole thing, the walking on egg shells in case you said the wrong thing and set them off, like the *'no'* word–especially Leon.

He'd only been with us three months, another of those short-term placements, another foster breakdown. The foster family wanted him back home, but Leon said no, he wanted to stay at Acorn House.

His real mother was a drunk, living with some drug-dealing jailbird and Leon had taken to spending a lot of time with her.

'So what's happening with dear, Leon?' I said.

'Still the same, still running with his mother's jailbird of a boyfriend,' said Shelly. 'My guess is he's supplying Leon with pot and other stuff, but we've no real proof and Leon's not singing. He's as loyal as a puppy, but not so cute.'

'Shelly, even if there was proof what could we do? Leon's running the show and like all the kids in here he knows it.'

'A referral has been made to Child and Adolescent Metal Health Services for some therapeutic intervention to begin, but Leon's declined to participate,' said Margaret. 'He scares me.' Margaret gave a little shiver and closed her eyes.

'So who's on tonight?' I asked.

'Tonight, lovely, James is your team leader and Mary's back after her annual leave,' said Shelly.

I pushed Leon to the back of my mind. 'How's Mel been?'

'Not good. We had a bastard of a shift last night.'

I sat down and gave Shelly my full attention. Shelly related the details of the previous shift. Mel had been complaining of stomach pains and feeling sick most of the evening. In the end the pain got so bad staff took her to the local A&E.

'God, she was terrible at the hospital, swearing and screaming at the nurses. They wanted her to stay in.'

'And…' I said.

'She refused.'

'For fuck's sake, she's thirteen. How the fuck can she refuse?' I snapped the words out and right away was sorry.

Shelly shrugged her shoulders and leaned back in her chair. 'What can you do, it's up to her.' It was a gentle rebuke but I deserved more, much more.

I let out a deep sigh. 'Yeah I know. I'm sorry.'

'Shall I make a cup of tea?' asked Margaret, getting up and heading for the door. It broke the tension and I welcomed it.

'So what was it Shell?'

Shelly twisted her face, as if she'd tasted something unpleasant. 'Chronic faecal impaction.'

'What's that?'

'It's when you're bunged up.'

'Is that what the smell is?'

'It must be. What else would smell like…well like shit?'

My first thought was, 'more fucking paper work,' but then I thought about the poor kid and the pain she must have been in. At least now we knew what the horrible smell was and could deal with it. I couldn't believe they hadn't made a thirteen-year-old child stay in.

'They gave her medication,' added Shelly getting up to unlock the drugs cabinet, 'Something called 'M-O-V-I-C-O-L,' she pushed her glasses back up onto her head. 'But, she's refused to take it, says it tastes like shit.'

‘She’d know.’ As soon as I’d said it I hated myself, felt ashamed for making such a terrible joke. ‘So where is she now?’

‘At her mum’s; Carol and the social worker thought her mum might be able to persuade her to take the medication. Carol took advice from higher management first.’

One thing was for sure, Carol, must have thought it was serious to contact the higher ups for advice.

***

Chapter 17

'Did you write this?' said Carol.

I looked at the sheet of paper in front of me and I should have known better, but I gave her what she was looking for anyway.

'It's got my name on it.'

'Do you mind if I just read out what you've written here?'

'Be my guest.'

Leon was on the roof most of the night, staff requested that he come down,
but he declined. Staff explained the potential danger, but Leon declined, eventually Leon did come down from the roof.
When asked if he would be attending his educational placement in the morning, Leon became abusive to staff. Indeed, he was extremely belligerent insisting that he was unable to attend education, as he had no shoes.
Leon became even more hostile when staff offered to take him
To ASDA to purchase shoes for education.
Inappropriate language and aggressive behaviour followed. .

Carol looked up from the paper and seeing I had no response offered her own. 'Jerry, you can't use words like *hostile* or *belligerent* when writing the client diaries.'

'Why not?'

At first I thought she was pulling my leg, but her face was serious. In the two-and-a-half years I'd known Carol the speckles of grey in her hair had all but taken over and her once dark hair was on the retreat.

'Because,' she said, in a weary breath, 'children can't be hostile. They're just children.'

I should have shut up and nodded my head and said, '*yes you're right and I was out of order, how stupid of me,*' but I didn't. I couldn't believe what I was hearing. 'Try telling Mavis that,' I said.

Carol's face turned the colour of a blood orange and for a split second she was knocked out of her rhythm, but she was too much of an old pro, it was a momentary lapse and she quickly fell back on her manager pose. I pushed forward. I pulled the dictionary off the shelf, flicking its pages I read aloud.

'Carol, the word *hostile* is just an adjective, you know a describing word, meaning unfriendly and the word *belligerent* is another adjective simply meaning aggressive. And that's what happened. Leon was hostile and belligerent in his manner towards me. I was simply describing, with the use of adjectives, what happened.'

'But, it's not very child- centred language. Leon has a number of issues and he knows no other way of expressing himself. He has ADHD and oppositional defiant disorder.'

'Carol, with all due respect, he's a violent little twat. Outside of care he's an anti-social thug. In care, he's a vulnerable child. Why do we have to pathologise everything?'

Carol's face screwed up tight as a sailor's knot. She rubbed her hand through her hair, walked over to the window and adjusted the blind taking a moment to enjoy the sunshine. When she spoke it was soft and gentle. 'You could have been a team leader by now.'

'I just don't want it,' I said.

This subject came up from time to time and in truth, I had thought about it once, given it serious consideration but after the allegation I never wanted to shift lead again.

'It would develop you. The past is the past; you have to let it go. Embrace it, learn from it. Use it as a learning curve and move forward.'

'Carol, if I want to be developed I'll read a book.' It was a flippant reply.

Her gaze returned to the window. She glanced at her computer screen and closed down an e-mail she'd been writing. 'I'm talking as your friend now and not the manager of Acorn House. I've said it before and I'll say it again, you think too much. The system's not perfect, but we as carers have to work in it and do the best we can.'

By now I knew an olive branch when it was offered. Carol slumped down into her chair and I knew she didn't want to fight with me. She placed the client diary sheet on the table and I noticed how old her hands looked in the sunlight. At that moment all I longed for was to be out in the sunshine and full of whisky.

'So what do we do about Melissa?' I asked. The tension between us settled like a feather to the ground. It was a difficult subject on both our parts but it gave us the opportunity to move forward, to play manager and worker.

'I've spoken to Melissa's social worker, and she in turn has discussed it with her line manager, we both have. We think Melissa will benefit if she stays over at her mum's Friday till Saturday. We think it will make her more receptive to taking her medication.'

'Is the mother on board with this?'

'She is. We had a meeting with her yesterday and she fully supports us.'

I smiled. *So much for supervised contact,* I thought.

'Jerry, I know what you're thinking, but it's about working with Melissa, not against her and this is in her best interests.'

'If it works, fantastic. I'm just at a bit of a loss what to try this end.' It was true I was at a loose end and was open to anything at this point. I was also relieved that if this approach did work it was a big weight off my shoulders. 'It's just with her health problem and the shoplifting…I'm open to suggestions.'

Carol effortlessly glided into her behaviour modification toolbox producing an incentive plan. Within ten minutes I'd agreed to a star chart for good behaviour, with five gold stars securing a Freeview T.V. for Mel's room. For this Mel had to shower daily, attend school, settle at bedtime, be home by 9:30 and take her medication.

*

It catches you out like a good card trick the first time. It's what I imagine an old actor experiences when they catch a glimpse of themselves at a younger age on screen; the shock, the moment they realise they're not the same person they used to be.

After finishing an early shift I would be tired. Sometimes I would take to my bed early evening, overcome by not only a physical tiredness but something else, something the eye didn't catch.

Kate would take the full hit trying to follow a script she hadn't rehearsed.

'I've made you some tea, honey,' said Kate. 'Thought you'd be hungry when you got home. How was work?'

The question would be the blow out. Driving home I'd waited for that question, prayed for it. 'How was work?' Boom. It would begin.

'Let me ask you a question Kate. How would your day be if you had some little twat of a scum bag kid in your face all fucking day?'

I told her how Leon had a toy plastic double-barrel shotgun, which he stuck in the back of my head and followed me around for twenty minutes. I told her about his crazy mad laughing at my discomfort.

'I even closed myself in the office for ten minutes, but I can't stay in there all shift can I?'

Kate shook her head, her mouth tight.

'No I can't. I have to be on the shop floor with the other kids, supporting staff but when I came out he's right back at it. I sit down thinking, that'll defuse it, but the little cunt shoves the barrels right into my face.' I put two fingers on Kate's forehead to illustrate my point. 'I push the gun away but he just puts it back. I ask him to stop and he laughs and I want to take it and shove it up his arse sideways. James asks him to stop but Leon just laughs and all this time I have to stay calm and in control but inside I'm smouldering, burning.'

'Couldn't you just take it off him?' said Kate.

'Take it off him,' I laughed. 'If you so much as put your hands on him he'd shout for a complaints form. I mean how ridiculous does that sound, a plastic gun, but when you're there, when you're in it, its torture? Really, it's bullying because Leon knows there's nothing I can do.'

Kate placed her hand on my head, brushing back my hair.

'Then he started flicking his lighter at me.' I clicked my fingers. 'He threatened to set my hair on fire.' For a moment I was back in the room with Leon, his tiny mouth bursting wide into a grin. His bitten yellow fingernails thrust out in front of him, poking me in the chest chanting, 'You're a twat, Jerry, you're a twat.'

I looked up and saw that a red mark had formed on Kate's forehead where I had thrust my fingers. I felt ashamed.

'Why don't you go and have a lie down,' said Kate.

'Yeah, I think I will.'

Chapter 18

Mel had had no real education since the age of twelve; although bright, she had refused to go to school. She'd eventually, been allocated a place in a Pupil Referral Unit but this became untenable. The headmistress of the PRU, Ms Goodwin, hastily arranged a meeting in order to outline the path forward.

Ms Goodwin was speaking: 'Smelly Melly is what the children are calling her now.' Ms Goodwin smiled warmly, sympathetically. 'To be absolutely honest Melissa's behaviour whilst in school hasn't helped matters. She's prone to…shall we say…*hostile* behaviour.' When she spoke she looked first to Carol then to Laura Roberts and then to me making sure we were all on board. It appeared automatic, but it was a calculated approach, one I was sure she'd used many times before.

I looked towards Carol and couldn't help but smile. Carol didn't meet my gaze.

'Of course we don't condone bullying in any shape and we have attempted to use a process of restorative justice with one of the girls in question, but this never came off due to Melissa's lack of attendance. We have also made provision for Melissa to attend in a safe environment, she can work in the library… again Melissa has been somewhat…' she paused, whilst she searched for the appropriate word… 'uncooperative.'

Ms Goodwin struck the right balance, used the correct rhetoric; she manoeuvred with the skill of a Philadelphia lawyer. I looked to Carol, her concentration seemed intense but she looked tired, yet not for a minute fooled by the show of concern on Ms Goodwin's face. Carol was wise enough to know when she was beaten.

Ms Goodwin took a moment to let what she'd said rest and when sure there was no resistance, continued. Now her voice had lost all hesitation.

'This brings us to date. We had facilitated a reduced timetable with Melissa attending for one hour a day, two till three. A taxi was arranged to pick Melissa up and return her to Acorn House, but as you can see,' she handed each of us an attendance sheet, 'Melissa has only attended a total of 12 out of 118 sessions.'

Carol scanned the paper and shook her head in despair. I didn't bother to look at the printout I just fixed Ms Goodwin with a, 'what *now?'* look. She didn't miss a beat.

'This is of great concern to us, as I'm sure it is to you.'

Ms Goodwin hadn't put a foot wrong. She moved forward to the edge of her chair and for the first time her gaze wavered, it was only a flicker like a candle caught in a momentary draft and then it was full and bright again.

'Due to Melissa's ongoing health problem her needs may be better met with home tuition in order to support her through this difficult time.' There was no struggle from any of us. In truth I knew the outcome before I walked through the door. This was just the part where we went through the motions; where we did the dance. In care, meetings are like lottery tickets; the outcome is never what you wish for.

'Yes I have to agree. Melissa is not going to attend school and under the circumstances I don't see a problem with facilitating this.' It was the first time Laura Roberts had spoken throughout the whole meeting, up until this point; she'd sat, quietly, making notes. Perhaps preparing a defence I thought, but I was wrong. She too knew the script.

Laura Roberts had arrived 20 minutes late proclaiming, 'Busy day today, busy day.' She clutched her diary tight as if it was a valuable silk purse, her long lemon hair reflecting the sunshine that beamed through the window.

'I'll contact Paul Miller; he's the educational social worker, to arrange home tuition from the complementary education service. I'll also see if we can get a laptop for Melissa.' said Laura Roberts.

It had all been pleasant enough, professional on all levels. No great strain just the business of the day.

‘Must dash, busy day today,’ said Laura Roberts, heading out the door, her lemon hair bouncing.

*

Monday morning the Ofsted man called for an unannounced inspection that we all knew about two weeks before. Staff attempted to make light conversation, but he was having none of it. He inspected each file like an old professor going over his formulae in a laboratory one last time, making sure the quantities of samples were all accounted for and logged: the fire drill, medicine book, logged and recorded; client diaries; counsellor visits; menus; physical intervention/ restraint book, one page per child to provide confidentiality; reward and sanctions book. A pause while Matt searched for the admissions and discharges book. There was another book, one where staff recorded the amount of cannabis used by the children and the sanctions given. Under orders from higher management this was kept secret.

Margaret flitted in and out of the office like a little humming bird, scared she’d miss something, but afraid the Ofsted man would ask her a question.

When asked a question I was a professional coward. I'd been warned in advance by Carol to keep my opinions to myself. I couldn't say the kids didn't *do* school or that Mel was allowed to decline medical treatment.

OFSTED man toured the building; admired the plants and the new sofa. He seemed pleased. He checked one of the bedrooms with the permission of Terry, the only kid in. Terry complained about the flickering ceiling light in his bedroom, I nodded and said I would get Ted, the handyman, to repair it.

OFSTED man checked out the front of the building and tutted about the array of cigarette stumps that littered the front step like ants crawling over a rotten apple.

'It's the kids smoking on the front step,' I said. 'We ask the kids to clean it up, make it respectable.'

He made a quick note in his little pad.

He stopped to admire several sunflowers and I told him that the kids had grown them for a competition to see who could grow the tallest. It was a lie. The staff had really grown them, as the kids couldn't be bothered, but it all looked good for the inspection.

In all he stuck around for three long days and when he was gone Carol breathed a deep sigh of relief and said: 'I just hope we get a good or at least a satisfactory rating. Below and they can close us down and that means job losses.'

Two weeks later in a staff meeting, Carol told us we could no longer ask the kids to clean up the cigarette stumps from the front step, as OFSTED had stated it was degrading for the kids to do this. A stunned silence, cold as steel, hung in the air while we all waited for the punch line. There wasn't one.

Someone hesitantly brought up the staff sleep-in room. The resource manager, Victoria Grey, on a recent visit had decided the original staff sleep- in room was far too nice and should be given to a kid.

'The reason the staff sleep- in room is nice is because the staff keep it nice. The kid's rooms all look like tips because the kids won't keep them tidy,' said Shelly.

'Yeah and the mattress in the staff room has a big hole in it, so you can't even get a good nights kip,' said Matt.

I could see Carol knew they were right, but she had her orders.

'Also, with the old room you had your own bathroom and toilet; now you have to come out and cross the landing every time you need the loo,' said Shelly.

'I sympathise, but it's the children that are priority,' said Carol.

I looked around at the staff and I could see not one of them was willing to take a stand. Taking the silence as agreement Carol picked up the agenda. I couldn't resist.

'It's not a matter of priority Carol. It's a matter of equality. Otherwise what are we teaching the kids?' I said.

People were nodding their heads in agreement and Carol was about to defend her corner until I added, 'You want the staff to give good care to the kids, right?'

Carol nodded.

'Then how is that possible if staff can't even get a good night's sleep?'

A long discussion ensued and Carol finally agreed Matt could purchase a new mattress for the sleep-in room.

The meeting continued. Another round of tea and coffee was brought in and people squabbled over the importance of consistency: how many bags of crisps at supper should the kids be allowed or should it just be a choice between toast and cereal? It was Margaret who brought the proceedings back to the agenda.

'What are we going to do about Rebecca?'

Rebecca was a sec 20 and had been with us for two months. She and her mother didn't get on and the mother point-blank refused to have Rebecca back home.

'She's sixteen now and is meant to be on shared care spending two nights a week at her mother's, but some weekends she goes and on other weekends she refuses- I mean declines,' said Margaret.

'What was the original reason Rebecca came into care?' asked Matt.

'She stole her mother's mobile phone and her mum threw her out,' said Margaret.

'That's a valid reason for being in care?' asked Matt.

'Apparently,' I said.

'Its difficult,' said Carol, 'because if we push too hard the mother will just sever all ties and we don't want that.'

'I agree with Carol,' I said.

Carol was smiling, happy I was in support until I added, 'the real question should be not what we should do, but what *can* we do. The mother's got us over a barrel and she knows it.'

Carol fixed me with a disapproving look.

I looked around the room and checked the faces. At least Matt was smiling.

*

The journey back from the clinic was one of long silences. I felt stressed and was at a loss what to do next. I felt relieved we were in a hackney cab and the driver couldn't smell Melissa, due to the Perspex partition. The worst bit had been the little boy, the one who'd been playing, sliding the coloured beads over a spaghetti junction of wires connected to a large wooden play box, asking his mum what the smell was. 'Mummy, have you trumped?'

I pretended I didn't hear him.

*

The nurse was kind and gentle with Mel. She'd one of those chiming voices, the kind designed to put kids at ease. She had taken Mel to have her weight checked whilst I waited.

'All done,' said the nurse, indicating for Mel to take a seat. I wondered if the nurse was overcome by the smell, but if she was she was far too professional to let it show.

The doctor was reviewing some notes when we walked in, Mel's notes I imagined. She tapped on her keyboard glancing at the computer screen and then back to the paper in front of her. She was a petite woman. Her features smooth. There were few signs of ageing other than a few strands of greying hair.

'Hello. I'm Dr. Rayner, how do you do?'

Mel made no acknowledgment, she just stared ahead.

I broke the moment. 'My name is Jerry—I'm Mel's keyworker.'

Dr. Rayner looked puzzled.

'Mel lives in a children's home,' I said.

Dr. Rayner went back over her notes nodding to herself as she did so. 'Yes I see,' she said. 'So Mel,' she waited before continuing, checking it was okay for her to call her Mel, 'you came to A and E three weeks ago and you were diagnosed with,' she went back to her papers, 'chronic constipation and you were suffering from tummy pain?' She looked from Mel and then to me.

I nodded.

'So, how have you been? You were prescribed, Movical?' Again she dipped back into her notes.

'Yes,' I answered.

'So, how are you feeling Mel?' Dr. Rayner asked.

'Fine, fine, fine,' said Mel in the register of a tiny child's voice you'd think was about five. This, of course, was not true. Mel had not been fine.

'Excuse me doctor. That's not exactly true.'

I had the doctor's attention now. Mel sent me a hurt look that said *traitor*. I pushed on.

'We have been having some difficulty getting Mel to take her medication, she doesn't like the taste and the stomach pains have become more frequent.'

'No, no Mel you must take the medication on a regular basis or you won't get well. Do you understand?' said the doctor.

I looked towards Mel. Her eyes were closed and her head tilted back as if she was straining to hear something far away.

'I see,' Dr. Rayner said, taking a deep breath. 'May I examine your tummy?'

Mel let out a long drawn irritable breath. 'No.'

The doctor looked to me, as if I had the magic key. I picked up my cue. 'Come on Mel,' I said patiently. 'Let the doctor examine you.'

'Noooooo. No, no, no,' she said, slapping her hands on her thighs in rhythm with her answer.

I turned back to the doctor. I felt embarrassed by Mel's reaction. 'The thing is,' I said slowly, 'Mel has had these pains and the…odour for around three or four months now and it's of some concern.'

I could see Dr. Rayner was finding the whole situation perplexing, as for a brief moment the colour in her cheeks increased.

'You see, if she's not taking the medication,' she looked at Mel, but Mel was pretending to read the posters on the wall, 'then the bowel is not releasing the backlog of faeces.' She waited to see if what she'd said registered with Mel. 'What I'll do is prescribe a medication called Mebeverine to ease her bowel spasms.' The doctor turned to Mel, 'this will help ease your tummy pains.'

'Can we go now?' uttered Mel.

'In a moment Mel,' I said. I turned my attention back to the doctor. 'This has been going on for some time now and I just wondered, without being rude, if perhaps there was another reason for Mel's condition?' If she was insulted by this she didn't show it. She dipped back into her notes,

'No you're quite right to be concerned.' She turned the pages until she found what she was looking for. 'Both blood and urine tests came back negative.' She turned to the nurse, 'Perhaps we can repeat the blood and urine samples again.'

Mel was suddenly animated. 'No. I want to go home.'

The doctor made a decision not to push things, she could see if she did Mel would resist. 'I think next time then. In the meantime you must take your medication.' She turned to her computer and printed out a prescription for the Mebeverine and handed it to me. 'Please make an appointment for three weeks' time and it would be helpful if staff could keep a diary of Mel's bowel habits and bring it to clinic next time.'

I hope I didn't let my dismay show. A picture came into my head of staff waiting outside the toilet scribbling down Mel's shit pattern, of staff asking Mel, 'was that a number two or a number one?' If the other kids got hold of that it would be a nightmare for Mel. They'd already started calling her Smelly Melly.

'Yes, I will see if we can keep a record,' I said.

*

I studied Mel, her head still against the taxi window, as she stared out, watching, but seeing nothing. She looked frail, transparent like the grey outline of a ghost caught in a photograph.

I thought she must know all was not well with her body. Why wouldn't she just take the medicine? Why wouldn't she let the doctor examine her? Perhaps she couldn't mentally or emotionally see the danger she was in, let alone make a rational decision.

***

Chapter 19

'I tell yer, if that little bastard FODs me one more time I'm gonner kill him,' I said.

James looked up from the petty cash receipts.

'Its fucking assault that. If we did that to them they'd be right on to the children's complaints officer and we'd be suspended on the spot,' I said. I threw my car keys in the drawer and slammed it shut.

James placed the petty cash tin to one side; his large grey eyes came to rest on me. 'Yes, he's got problems, poor Leon.' James rubbed his knee.

'Nothing that a good fucking slap wouldn't cure.'

James ignored my rage and continued rubbing his knee. 'Leon's an extremely damaged young boy. Have you read his background?'

I took a deep breath; 'It's the fucking care system. It allows *them* to do what they want when they want with no fear of any consequences. It doesn't help the kids, it destroys them. That's why when they leave here they can't cope. That's why they end up in prison or homeless.'

'I don't agree.'

'You don't agree? This isn't just my opinion, look at the stats. The outcomes for these kids are horrendous.'

He shook his head. He looked like a school teacher chastising a small boy for running in the corridor.

'You need to forget about the system. You're not going to change it. But I think if you can change just one child,' he held up a lone nicotine finger, 'that child may go on to change the world.' His finger stayed there a whole breath after he'd made his point.

'I admire your optimism and I think we do change kids,' I said.

A smile broke across James's face.

'But for the worst.'

James's smile retreated. 'Yes, well I care about the kids.'

'From my observations I don't think it makes any discernible difference to outcomes whether you care or not, as long as you just do your job.'

James's eyes narrowed and his face became stern and serious. 'If anyone is here just for the money, as far as I'm concerned they shouldn't be here.'

'Ninety percent of the population are in jobs just for the money,' I said. How dare James preach that idealistic shit. He was always here for the money, doing more hours than all of us and using his *collective responsibility* banner as justification.

There was an uncomfortable silence and when James spoke his voice took on a gentler tone. 'Have you ever heard the story of the starfish?'

I shook my head, more in amusement than anything else.

James shuffled his chair from behind the desk stopping opposite me like a teacher getting ready to read a story to a class of young children.

'There are thousands of starfish washed up on the beach and a boy no more than nine is going along picking each one up and throwing them back in the sea.'

While recounting the story James played the part of the young boy, miming flinging imaginary starfish into an imaginary sea. 'An old man seeing him doing this, asks him why? There's thousands. You can't possibly save them all says the old guy.' James was now playing the part of the old man, his eyes wide and bemused by the wonder of it all.

'The small boy says, 'yes' but I can save this one and I can save this one.' Again James held up an imaginary starfish and mimed throwing it into his pretend ocean.

He looked at me smiling, happy with his allegory. He sat back, folded his arms watching to see how this struck me. For my part, I let out a long tired breath.

'James, these aren't starfish, they're people. The starfish weren't resisting the little boy's help, unlike dear little Leon. I mean we can't even make him go to school. Education is one of our, if not our biggest areas of failure. I mean how many kids after they come in here just stop going to school?'

James shifted his weight in the chair and rubbed his knee. 'These are damaged children that find it difficult to engage with school.'

'Oh bollocks and you know it. They all end up in *alternative education*, sitting off all day playing pool, but as long as the local authority can say they're in some form of *education* it looks good on paper. They're fucking kids. Choices are fine, but some choices should not be open to discussion like whether or not a kid goes to school.'

'You can't make them do things, Jerry that would be authoritarian. I didn't want to go to school when I was a kid. And why should they take notice of us old fogies?'

I stood up and leaned across the desk, weary of the battle now. 'That's fine,' I said, 'but at some point someone has to be the adult or this,' I spread my arms indicating Acorn House, 'is what we get. And what about Mel, how long do we allow her the *choice* to be treated or not, as the case is? When all is said and done, she's just a child.'

James' blew out his cheeks like a puffer fish, his breath ruffling the paper on the desk in front of him. 'It's…it's a difficult case,' he said, rubbing his knee.

*

I began to find it increasingly difficult to shake off the despair and depression I felt whenever I was in work. It would be there when I awoke each day, growing out of control like a neglected garden.

Millie came skipping into the room, chatting about her day in school and telling how her PE teacher praised her for the long-jump. Laughing, sweet as a pea, as she told us Emily Harris had fallen, legs and arms flying everywhere. I was in the thick of it attempting to have a conversation with Kate that was becoming repetitive.

'Kate, I just hate my job.'

Kate was busy emptying Millie's lunch box. 'Millie, you didn't eat your apple again.'

Millie stopped her chatting. 'Sorry mum.'

'I tell you I'm going to end up killing that little twat Leon.'

Kate stared at me. 'Can we have this conversation later, not in front of Millie, hey?'

Millie didn't appear to care. She opened the fridge and took a large gulp of milk.

'We have no rights. The kids can treat us anyway they want. Take that little bastard Leon he—'

'Jerry!' Kate looked at Millie.

'Okay.' I began again keeping my voice calm and low. 'Take Leon, he keeps coming up and foding me and I can't—'

'Foding?'

'Yes. Foding.' I demonstrated with my open palm, gently, on Kate's forehead. 'And it hurts.'

'That didn't hurt,' she said, laughing.

'That's because,' I said, I could feel the frustration rising in me, 'that's because I'm doing it gently. When Leon does it, he does it with purpose. And he's using it to target me.'

'Well report him.'

'Report him. Report him,' I said in disbelief. 'Do you ever listen to me?' My voice was raised now. 'All Carol will say is that it's part of our job to deal with *challenging behaviour.*'

'What do you want me to do Jerry?'

'I want you to—'

'Mum, can I play out for a bit?'

'Millie! We're talking,' I snapped.

Millie stopped, frozen to the spot, her blue eyes filled with hurt.

Kate glared at me. 'Alright, that's enough.'

'Millie,' she said calmly. 'Make sure your uniform is ready and hung up for tomorrow and then you can play out.'

I felt ashamed for having snapped at Millie.

I waited till Millie went upstairs. 'I just want you to understand what I'm going through. I can't do this job much longer.'

'Well then quit.'

'For fuck's sake how can I quit? I have a mortgage to pay, a responsibility to you and Millie, perhaps if we weren't in so much fucking debt.'

'Oh, so it's my entire fault?' Kate slammed her hands down on the table. 'You said it was okay, that we could have some nice things now you were working. We discussed this Jerry. I just did what we agreed. I ask you again, what do you want me to do?'

From up stairs came the faint sound of Millie singing. I lowered my voice. 'You know, I'm working with a thirteen-year-old girl and I just know the kid's real sick, but they're just allowing her to drift. They're meant to protect and nurture. God, they talk about protecting kids from adults when they can't even protect kids from themselves.'

She moved towards me and put her arms around me. 'I love you, but you have to stop this. You're bringing it home with you and I won't allow you to take it out on me, and especially Millie.'

She broke away from the embrace. 'What's happened to you? You used to be so carefree. People are always saying, 'oh he's great your husband, such a good laugh, always joking.' God if only they knew.'

I sank into the chair, deflated. 'I just get so depressed. It's the fucking kids, they wear you out. I'm so tired of being treated like a lower form of life. It's the fucking system.'

Kate put her hands on my shoulders. 'But don't treat us that way. Don't *become* them, just be a decent person. What else can you do?'

My head fell into my hands and I began to weep.

Melissa was not taking her medication. This was clear. Carol's star chart hadn't worked and home tuition had been a bad, but well intended disaster.

Monday: 9:30: 'Are you getting up, Mel, your home tutor is here?'

'No, not feeling well.'

Tuesday: 9:30: 'Come on, Mel, your teacher will be here soon, get yourself up and ready.'

'Fuck off.'

Wednesday: 9:30: 'Come on, Mel, you only have to do one hour. She's downstairs waiting. At least give her a chance. She seems really nice.'

'Fuck off! I'm not well.'

And so the script went. Mornings were changed to afternoons, as it was recognised perhaps mornings were not the best time for Mel, but the pattern continued. The laptop that had been provided for Mel was lost.

'Left it on the bus Jerry, Jerry,' said Mel smiling. 'Do yer like me new phone?'

*

Linda Evans, the Looked After Nurse for Children in Care (LAC), visited Mel, to try and persuade her to take her medication, but she remained unco-operative. Mel's social worker, Laura Roberts visited, took Mel for a MacDonald's in an effort to get her to see the light. Laura asked me to tag along.

'*Please* Melissa,' she pleaded. 'You won't get better if you don't take your medicine.'

'It tastes horrible,' Mel insisted.

'But if you don't take it, Melissa, you won't get well. You know what the doctor said.'

'I hate doctors. I don't care, I wanner die,' said Mel, as if she was a ham actor in some old horror film.

That night Mel's medication was mixed into some sweet and sour chicken without her knowledge, a raindrop in an ocean of chaos. After this the medication was mixed into cans of Vimto to disguise the taste. Mel agreed to this, but only if Carol agreed to a twenty pounds incentive. Another twenty was promised but only if Mel attended a Child and Adolescent Metal Health appointment.

Chapter 20

I opened Mel's file and logged that the Child and Adolescent Mental Health appointment had taken place.

'How did it go?' James's voice cut into my thoughts.

'Shit,' I said.

I must have looked more depressed than usual because James had lost that preaching religious smiling look. It was now replaced by a look of real concern for my well-being. He dragged his bad leg around the desk. 'Did she cooperate with CAMHS?'

I slumped heavily into a chair and observed James. He looked older today.

'Not in the least.' The words sounded as weary as I felt and I thought 'what the hell,' maybe James could come up with a different angle. 'She just...she just sits there whilst Jenny Kesey, the CAMHS lady, asks her how she feels. In the end I went outside whilst this Kesey woman did her child psychology stuff, but nothing's moving that's for sure, bowels wise or otherwise.'

James took a moment to close a window before he spoke. 'She's good Jenny, she knows her stuff, a nice woman.'

I rubbed my eyes and took a deep soothing breath. 'I'm sure she is, but do you know what she said to me?'

James sat forward like he was waiting for me to pull the rabbit out the hat.

'She asked if I thought Mel might be imagining it.' I started to laugh.
'*Imagining it,* can you believe that?'

James said nothing, he just listened.

'Anyway, I ask *Ms Kesey* if she could smell the *odour* coming from Mel or were we all just imagining it.'

James was still for a moment and then he said, 'Perhaps she meant imagining it in a psychological sense, that she's holding onto her bowels and not going the toilet due to some emotional trauma. Perhaps…' he hesitated measuring the beat of his words, making sure he had my full attention, 'perhaps Jenny suspects sexual abuse. I know I do.'

I hadn't meant to snap but I did. 'Yeah, and it's probably the mother's boyfriend, but we still let her go and visit her mother and stay over. How can that be right?'

He didn't answer. Not for the first time that day I felt I was seeing the world from a half-way sleep. I just wanted to be at home and drift away, to be filled with a numbness that no one could reach.

'No, it's not right but, if it helps, the mother called today and said that she wants no more overnight stays for Mel due to the smell.'

'Yeah, but she'll still go round there. Some mother, hey?' I laughed.

'Anyway, Ms Kesey is going to arrange for Mel to be seen by a consultant in child and adolescent psychiatry to ascertain Mel's mental health and emotional well-being. If a case can be argued that Mel is incapable of making the right decision they could, I guess, section her under the Mental Health Act. That way she'd have no choice but to be treated.'

10:30 am: I was sitting with Mel having informed the receptionist we were here to see Jenny Kesey. It took a ten pound top-up for Mel's mobile to get her to attend the appointment. Mel, her hair un-brushed, looked weak and washed out. She sat with her arms folded across her stomach, her face tight against the pain. She smelt like a damp room.

The door opened and Jenny Kesey waved us through. 'Hello Melissa - I mean Mel. See I remembered,' she laughed.

We all laughed apart from Mel. We sat down.

'This is Dr. Angela Carter and she's going to ask you a few questions.' We were met by a rather attractive black lady with a beaming smile.

'Hello Mel,' Dr. Carter extended her hand.

'Hello,' murmured Mel.

The Doctor turned her attention towards me. 'You are?'

'I'm Jerry— Mel's keyworker.' I put out my hand.

'Welcome, Jerry.'

Jenny Kesey was smiling, always smiling, hovering in the background like a magician's assistant.

'Okay Mel,' said Dr. Carter, 'I'm just going to ask you a few questions so that we can have a little chat. Are you okay with that? Remember you're in control.'

Mel gave a slight nod.

'Okay, so how are you feeling today?'

'Fine.'

If the smell had hit Dr. Carter she did a good job of hiding it. I was impressed. Dr. Carter leaned forward. 'I'm told you've been in some pain recently? How are you today?'

'Fine.'

'Have you been taking your medication?'

Mel grinned. She began to rock back and forth, her arms tightening around her stomach. Dr. Carter flashed me a look. I took it as my cue.

'No she hasn't taken her medication regularly, it's been quite sporadic.'

Suddenly Mel began to cry. A solitary tear traced its way down her cheek. There was no sobbing. No sound escaped her lips, just a silent tear drop. She stared straight ahead.

Dr. Carter sat back in her chair.

Jenny Kesey came forward and placed one hand on Mel's knee.' Mel are you in pain? Would you like a glass of water?'

There was no reply, only that far off stare as if Mel could see something approaching in the distance the rest of us were blind to.

'Mel,' I said, 'we only want to help you, but you have to tell us babe, what's wrong? Let us help you.'

She tilted her head to one side and for a moment she looked so lost, so helpless that I wanted to embrace her and tell her not to get upset, it would be okay.

'Jerry's right, Mel, let us help you,' said Jenny Kesey, her voice soothing and warm, but it had no impact.

Dr. Carter was studying Mel and if I didn't know better I would have thought she was uncomfortable with the whole situation, but I reasoned she must see this sort of thing all the time. Perhaps I was just being over- sensitive, but as I watched Mel I made a decision.

'Okay, that's enough,' I said. 'She's upset so I think we'll go. You okay with that Mel?'

Mel nodded.

Dr. Carter looked to Jenny Kesey, but we were already up and heading for the door, my hand gently guiding Mel out.

'Yes…yes…I think that would, at this time, be for the best,' said Jenny Kesey as we strode out.

*

We entered a café in the indoor shopping centre. It had just gone lunch time, but there were still a number of people on extended lunch breaks, a few ties and suits but mostly elderly ladies out for a spot of gossip and warm soup. I left Mel at a table in the far corner while I got the drinks. I placed a mug of hot chocolate in front of Mel. She cupped it with both hands, carefully, slurping the hot liquid, studying the room over the rim of the mug. Not satisfied with the taste she put the mug down and picked up three of the sugar sachets and gently tore at the edge of each one carefully adding the granules to her drink.

'Sweet enough for you?' I asked. 'You okay now?'

She shot me a smile. For a moment we just sat watching the people go about their day; people at tables immersed in their newspapers, reading a book or absorbed in their phones. I felt so sorry for Mel during the meeting and I was genuinely surprised at my response, but something in me, perhaps a paternal instinct, if there is such a thing, reacted and I just needed to get Mel out of there.

As I looked across at her now I couldn't help but wonder what if this was my daughter. I pictured Millie's bright face, full of joy, secure in her world of loving parents. I tried to imagine what my daughter would be like if she'd spent her young life in care. She would no doubt have been as devastated by her short life, as the fractured child in front of me. I caught the conversation of two elderly ladies battling with their shopping trolleys and the arrangement of their chairs,

'Oh dear, what is that smell?'

'Must be the drains, dear.'

‘I hope it’s not the soup.’

If Mel heard the comment she made no response, she just sipped her chocolate. I made an attempt at conversation. I didn’t want to proceed too quickly and scare her off. Mel was too shrewd for that. My approach had to be measured, well paced.

We talked about Mel’s mother. I asked how contact had been going. There was a truth in her eyes when she said, all she really wanted was for her and Lizzy to go back home to mum.

‘I miss Lizzy,’ she said.

While I was sure that one day she would return home, *didn’t they all drift back eventually?* it wouldn’t be the way she played it out in her fantasies of family life.

All this, of course, was just circling around the issue, looking for an opening.

’Has the pain gone?’ I asked.

Mel nodded.

‘Mel, can I just say, I don’t know what your problem is, but whatever it is we can help, if you’ll just let us find out what’s causing it.’

She carefully placed her mug in front of her and picked up the salt shaker and began turning it around in her hand. Touching the top with her finger and placing the tip into her mouth grimacing at the bitter taste.

'Jerry.'

I leaned forward. 'Yes, Mel.'

'You know I lent Leon two bifftas yesterday and he said that when he gets a packet today he would give me three. Well he better or I'll take it out of his face.' She held her fist up to make her point but she was smiling.

'Well don't lend bifftas or better still, don't smoke.'

'Does your kid smoke?'

'No. And I wouldn't let her. Anyway, how long do you plan to keep going on like this?'

'Lending bifftas?'

'You know what I mean.' For a moment I expected an off the wall response, another attempt at distraction.

'I know what's wrong with me.'

I felt my chest tighten. I had to go real careful now. Too fast and it would scare her off like a baby doe.

'Yeah, so how long have you had this medical degree of yours?' I spoke the words flippantly, trying to draw her in.

'I just know that's all.'

'Pray tell, Dr Mel, what's your diagnosis?' I kept it light. Perhaps standing up for her in the meeting had secured a little bit of trust and a little bit of trust was all I needed.

'I can't say.'

I was losing her. She'd crept back into the dark, ready to bolt.

'What do you think happens when you die?'

I took a mouthful of tea. 'Nothing, we die and that's that. Why?'

'My mum said she saw my nan's ghost.'

I drained the last of my tea. 'You can tell me anything. If there's something worrying you, trust me, there's nothing I haven't heard and nothing we can't deal with.'

'I can't say.'

'Why?'

'You'll report it.'

She was at the edge of the darkness now, another moment and she'd be hidden back inside. But she was right and I couldn't lie to her, it would be unethical.

'Yes. You're right, I would have to report it because it's my job.'

I watched her drain the last remnants of chocolate from the mug before placing her arms across her waist, her face sallow and distant.

***

Chapter 21

In the middle of all this chaos Mel's review meeting was held. I asked Mel to fill out a consultation document but she shook her head and said: 'Reviews are a waste of time, no one listens.'

I gave Mel the whole spiel about the importance of having her voice heard. I almost convinced myself, but she wouldn't bend.

The review generated a Specific Issues Meeting at which I got the opportunity to address the decision-makers. I spoke calmly and to the point.

'There's no other way to say this but Mel has started soiling herself and frequently. Then there's the foul smell, the weight loss, the stomach pains so severe Mel often sobs, and when we offer to take her to the doctors or A&E she becomes upset, even violent'

A few of the decision-makers even managed to look up from their notes. I pushed on, the blood rushed up my neck and into my face and I lost control.

'She's a thirteen-year-old child, if she was laid out there now with a broken leg we wouldn't be giving her the choice to be treated or not, we'd just treat her. If this was your own kid would you let her dictate like this?'

Carol gave me a reassuring smile.

It was the reviewing officer that spoke. He never looked at me. He focused his narrow eyes on Carol and Laura Roberts. 'I think that having reviewed the case it's evident that this…constipation will…'

'What if it's not constipation? What if it's something else?' I said.

Carol looked at me, her smile gone.

'As I was saying,' continued the reviewing officer, 'as Dr. Rayner has stated, if Melissa takes her medication regularly then the constipation will improve.' He leaned forward in his chair, his voice attempting to convey a little compassion, 'Of course this is an emotional situation, but we have to, all of us,' he looked intently, right at me, 'act in a professional manner.' He sat back pleased with himself. 'Perhaps, if Melissa doesn't respond to the taste of the medication we could ask Dr.

Rayner to prescribe a similar acting medication, one with a more pleasant taste. In the meantime, I would advocate keeping a dialogue open with CAMHS and continued monitoring of the situation.'

The reviewing officer tipped his head and looked through the bottom of his glasses and checked his notes.

'I note that Dr. Carter, the consultant in child and adolescent psychiatry, was unable to do a full examination of Melissa but this may still be an avenue open to us in the future. Until then much depends on Melissa's level of co-operation.'

I was stunned at this feeble response. A few polite goodbyes and rattling of teacups and the meeting came to a close.

*

It was two days before I managed to corner Carol.

'Carol, all I want is your permission to write to Dr. Rayner and request a surgical opinion, as well as a change of medication, as suggested at the meeting. I just want to cover all the bases. I mean what if it's not this…chronic…faecal impaction constipation thingy?'

I sat on the edge of Carol's desk. She looked at me contemplating her answer. Her thin lips broke into a half-smile.

'Yes. Do that. I guess it's only good practice.'

I told Matt my intentions. His response lit a fire of worry in me I didn't expect. 'Just make sure you log everything and cover your arse, mate.'

My reply came three weeks later:

Dear Mr—
Melissa is a 13-year-old girl currently being treated for faecal impact/chronic constipation. She currently attends clinic for this and is prescribed Movicol to aid in, what I suspect, is a back log of faeces. I have also prescribed Mebeverine for the discomfort of bowel spasms associated with constipation. In light of Melissa's reluctance to take her medication I would suggest a change of medication (although movicol remains the best option) in place of the movicol: Docusate Sodium 100mg capsules four times daily. A prescription for this can be provided by Melissa's GP.

I also request that staff at Acorn House keep a diary of Melissa's bowel habits. I fully understand the problematic nature of such a request, but it is necessary if we are to reach a decision on how best to manage the constipation. I note that at the beginning of July Melissa attended A&E and on this occasion was seen by Mr. McCann's surgical team and was treated for constipation, before discharging herself. Therefore, whilst I understand your concerns I do not think there is any indication for a further surgical re-referral.

In addition, I understand that Melissa has been resistant to further clinic appointments; therefore, I would suggest a multi-agency meeting as soon as possible to include all the relevant people to plan a way forward.

Yours sincerely

Dr. B. Rayner
Consultant Paediatrician.

cc Laura Roberts (Social worker).
cc Jenny Kesey (CAMHS).

Mel was on the sofa, her knees pulled up tight to her chest. She'd just gotten off the phone to her mother. Mel wanted to go round and see her mum but from the sullen look on her face I guessed the mother had made some excuse. I figured it was cider night at home.

'Everything all right, Mel?' I asked.

She looked at me with watery eyes and I wasn't sure if what I said registered. 'Are you out tonight?' I said.

I sat down opposite her and picked up the newspaper. I'd drunk a little too much whisky the night before and there was still the echo of a slight buzz in my head. Another fight with Kate had ended with me sleeping on the sofa. It was always the same lately.

'I hate my fucking job. I'm tired of getting told to fuck off for a living. I'm tired of working for a system that takes its lead from a 13-year-old child.'

'Then pack it in, Jerry, because I can't deal with this much longer,' Kate had yelled, her face distorted with pain, her blue eyes aflame.

I looked over the paper at Mel. She'd lost even more weight if that was possible and her hair looked dull and brittle. She was sitting there lost in thought, chewing at the ends of her hair before pulling at the tip of her tongue to remove the fine chewed bits.

It had been a week since Mel had started her new medication. It was now given in tablet form, and although she was taking the medication there had been little, if any, improvement, the odour still seeped out of every pore on her body. It made sitting in the same room as her almost unbearable. Added to my whisky hangover it was a bad mix. I got up to leave the room when the calm was broken by the drilling of the door bell. Leon.

He could see through the glass I was coming yet he still pressed on the door bell, his face squashed against the glass, grinning.

'Leon, you can see me coming why do you keep ringing the bell?'

He pushed past me. 'Who's in twat?'

'Just Mel. Do you have to use such language?' I said.

Leon shuffled into the living room jumping up and punching a picture frame on the way. 'Got any bifftas?'

'No.,' said Mel. 'Anyway, you owe me bifftas from the other week.'

Leon smiled and dropped down onto the opposite sofa both his hands down the front of his pants, even he wasn't stupid enough to sit too close.

'I've got money coming today and I'll pay yer back, he said. 'Jerry, I never got me pocket money yesterday cos I was missin Friday, but I can get it today can't I?'

'I don't know. You'll have to ask Shelly, she's the team leader.'

He jumped up off the sofa and knocked at the office door in one fluid movement. 'Shelly! Can I have me pocket money?'

Shelly's voice sprang back. 'Is your room tidy?'

'Yeah.'

'Get Jerry to check it then.'

Leon kicked the office door with his foot.

'Come on then,' I said. 'Let's see your room.'

Leon sniffed. 'It's not done yet.'

He turned back to Mel. 'Go on, Mel save us on half a biffta and I'll do me room and I'll buy some.'

'No,' said Mel.

'Go on?'

'No.'

'Fucking smelly bitch, you just wait!'

'Why don't yer go and get bummed, I hear yer like that!'

'Fuck off, dog shit face. Smelly Melly, smelly Melly,' Leon ranted like a twisted children's nursery rhyme.

Mel closed her eyes tight against the onslaught.

'Okay, Leon, that's enough,' I said. 'Go and tidy your room, get your pocket money and then you can get your own bifftas.'

Leon went into the dining room to the water dispenser and filled a plastic cup. He came back out and before I could figure what he was up to, he swilled Mel over the head with the water.

'Get a fucking wash, Smelly Melly.'

'Yer fucking bastard, bum boy,' screeched Mel. She got up and headed for the dining room.

Leon didn't run but retreated to the hallway out of range. 'Smelly Melly, Smelly Melly.'

Mel filled a cup with water.

I stepped in front of her. 'Come on Mel, Just let it go.'

'No. I'm gonna get that fucking nonce.'

Leon was now on the stairs his small mouth grinning, enjoying the chase. Mel was fired up intent on giving him a soaking.

Shelly stepped out of the office and looked to me for an explanation.

'It's Leon being a prat,' I said.

'Well if Leon wants his pocket money he'd better calm down and tidy his room.'

Shelly turned towards Mel. 'And you, young lady, you need to settle down right now.'

It was an attempt at being stern and for a brief moment it stopped Mel in her tracks. Leon was edging his way further up the stairs. Mel placed the cup onto the table and brushed past me.

'Where you off?' I said.

She looked up at Leon who had gone further up the stairs, but seeing Mel no longer had any water in her hand, stepped back down.

'For a biffta,' said Mel smiling.

I could see Leon was tempted but he thought twice and again headed up the stairs.

'Someone open me room,' came the shout.

'I'll go,' said Shelly.

Shelly came back down, blowing out her cheeks and rolling her eyes. 'You okay out here, Jerry while I finish up some paper work?'

'Yeah, no probs.'

Mel was standing on the front step one arm clutched tight to her waist. She gently moved from foot to foot whilst drawing on a cigarette.

'You okay Mel?'

She tilted her head towards me and screwed up her face. 'Yeah,' she said, blowing out smoke.

'Are you in pain?' I asked, indicating her stomach.

She kicked a ciggie stump off the step. 'J-e-r-r-y,' she spoke in a long drawn out almost musical breath. By now I knew when I was being side stepped. I went along anyway.

'Yes Mel, what can I do for you?'

'I haven't seen my little sister for months and that fucking social worker said she'd arrange contact, but has she fuck.'

Mel was only allowed supervised contact with her stepsister four times a year. Lizzy's foster family were convinced such meetings were having a detrimental effect on Lizzy and they felt Mel was doing her best to sabotage Lizzy's foster placement by putting bad ideas into her head. Mel told her social worker she'd witnessed the foster parents mistreating Lizzy. Lizzy didn't substantiate the claim. After an investigation found no substance to Mel's allegation the foster parents became wary of any future contact. I had to admit knowing this made me a little uneasy whenever I found myself alone with Mel.

'I'll phone Linda in the morning and check what's happening. How's your mum doing?'

'Fine.'

Mel's mother had only visited her at Acorn House, that I knew of, on two occasions and one of them was at Carol's urging. The other was when Mel received £150.00 clothing money. Mel's mother returned all embarrassed with only four items of clothing that never in a hundred years added up to £150.00 quid proclaiming, 'How daft am I? I lost the receipts.'

'Jerry, will you get me a drink of milk please?'

'Yeah sure.'

A slight shiver took hold of me. 'You better wrap up Mel. It's getting a little chilly.'

By the time I'd returned with the milk she was gone.

Leon reappeared, snorting and laughing at something that caught his fancy in the newspaper. He sprawled across the sofa but when he saw me approaching he sat up straight. 'Hey, Jerry, look at this picture here.'

I leaned forward to check out what it was he found so funny. When he saw I was in range he moved to FOD me. I pulled back just in time. I forced a smile. 'You're so funny Leon.' *Fuck,* I thought, *it never lets up just patterns repeating themselves over and over.*

Mel didn't come back for two days. She phoned up from her mother's house in pain and staff went to collect her. She refused to go to the hospital. As I said, just patterns playing over and over and over.

***

Chapter 22

I arrived for work at 2:20 pm. Matt, Carol, Margaret, Shelly, Mary and Lucy, the new girl, were all crowded into the office. Stillness permeated the room, a physical thickness in the air that I hadn't felt before. It was grief.

'James has died,' someone whispered, their voice unsteady.

'How?' I said.

'Heart attack,' said Carol in a hushed tone quiet as a prayer. 'He'd suffered from high blood pressure for a while and they think…' her voice lost its way.

I knew it. All the fucking hours the man put into this shithole thinking he could change the world. All the overtime, working three days and nights solid, chanting his mantra *'collective responsibility'* and where did it get him?

Dead.

'We're taking a collection if you want to put in?' said Matt.

'Yes, yes of course,' I said. Suddenly a thought entered my mind, a subject that for whatever reason never came up in our conversations. 'Did he have any family?' I asked.

'No. He lived on his own,' said Matt.

Poor James, he wanted to save the starfish but the effort sucked him dry. I looked across at Lucy, her mascara smeared across her young cheeks. I recalled her telling someone her father hadn't long passed away. I felt sorry for her because her grief must have still been raw.

Coupled with my sorrow at James's passing came a deep sense of guilt. Our last conversation had been a little heated and I'd been rather unkind in my comments.

*

We'd been having one of our many discussions and what started as light conversation took a bitter turn when we got onto the subject of kids in care having too many rights and us, the workers, being treated like second-class citizens by the authority and the kids. Of course, James disagreed.

'James, any one of those kids out there,' I said pointing towards the office door, 'has the power to destroy us and I should know.'

The mood seemed right so I told James of the allegation that had been made against me. I told him how it had wounded me emotionally; a wound that remained open to this day. How I couldn't forgive. It poured out of me, all the anger, all the despair. I stood before James open and raw, but I didn't care. I wanted James to know there was a valid reason for the way I was. Once I tried so hard to be like him, a saviour of starfish. If what I said unsettled James he didn't show it.

'You mustn't let it sour you.'

'It hasn't soured me,' I said through gritted teeth. 'It's made me a realist. I mean I didn't even get a fucking apology.'

The air between us was still for a moment, crisp.

'I had an allegation made against me once.'

'You had an allegation?' I said shocked.

'It was when I worked in another home. A kid said I hit him and I was suspended for six months, with pay. After an investigation I was fully exonerated. My point is I realised that it wasn't personal to me. The authority was just doing its job. What they had to do.'

'I bet they never apologised afterwards?' I said.

James shrugged his shoulders. 'Why should they apologise? An apology would have meant nothing to me. It was the kid, and he wouldn't apologise, he was too damaged. For all I know it may have been a cry for help because he didn't trust adults. I don't know.'

I looked him over, this man who only the other week had his car badly scratched and two of the tyres slashed by Leon for refusing him travel money, this man whom the authority didn't compensate for the damage. This man who when the authority said, *'You're not an essential car user,'* accepted it.

'Then I'm sorry James but you're a fool. Allegations destroy lives.'

Then I said something I will always regret. 'If you, God forbid, died tomorrow, this place would just roll on and these kids and the authority wouldn't give a flying fuck.'

When Carol told the kids of James's death, her voice soft as dust, there was a moment of silence, then, some uneasy laughter, perhaps hoping she was joking. There were no tears, but something did stir in them if only for a split second. I think even they felt vulnerable to death, even if it was only for a moment; they glimpsed their own mortality, at least until Mel shouted, 'Biffta.' There were a few, *'Oh my God, I can't believe it,'* comments but little real sadness. The news of James's passing didn't impinge on their world for long. How could it, no one had ever taught them about empathy. One of the kids asked would they still be able to go clothes shopping at the weekend and when that was sorted, life at Acorn House moved on.

Later we got the full story: Carol told us James had mentioned something about chest pains the day before. That night when he was at home the pains must have got bad because James knocked on a neighbour's door for help. The neighbour, thinking the banging and shouting was a drunk from the nearby pub, ignored his shouts. The neighbour eventually came out to find

James lying face down in the front yard. By time the ambulance arrived James was dead.

***

Chapter 23

We'd driven to the multi-agency meeting in Carol's car. Prior to leaving I'd taken some stick off Matt for wearing a suit. I told him it was important to look smart when representing the authority. Carol agreed and said it was a nice touch. Secretly, I thought wearing a suit might afford me some respect in a room full of professionals.

They were already sitting round a large oblong table when we arrived. Apart from myself, Carol, Linda Evans, Jenny Kesey and Dr. Rayner, there was one face I hadn't seen before. Dr. Rayner introduced her as Belinda Marshals, a play specialist assigned to the hospital.

Dr. Rayner gave a brief overview of Mel's case and then it was my turn to speak. I'd prepared myself for this moment, gone over it in my mind a thousand times and used the journey in the car to repeat the process. Despite all my preparation I gave a rather emotional account of the situation.

I spoke of the odour that was now so foul I believed it was having an impact on Mel's emotional well-being and self-esteem. I told of how Mel's education had broken down and explained Mel was the victim of bullying from other young people calling her Smelly Melly. At times my voice wavered, almost broke, but I'd planned for this. I paused, took a deep breath, and continued meeting each person's gaze as I spoke. I ended with the bold suggestion of a surgical opinion being the way forward and the choice to comply with this should be taken, once and for all, out of the *child's* hands.

Dr. Rayner observed me for a moment and straightened her papers. When she spoke her voice was soft but firm.

'Let me be clear where, I believe, we are up to in this matter. I suspect that Melissa is suffering from a backlog of faeces.'

I started to protest, but Dr. Rayner cut me short.

'True, I cannot be completely certain of this without examining her and she has, up to this point, been reluctant to allow this.' Dr. Rayner waved her hand indicating Belinda. 'This is where Belinda comes in.'

Belinda Marshal picked up her cue. 'I shall arrange to visit Melissa at Acorn House and take time to get to know her, gain her confidence.' Belinda didn't move when she spoke, she stayed perfectly posed. Her, palms turned down on the table in front of her. Her nails clipped to a point, her smart dark blue suit wrinkle-free. 'It would be an immeasurable help if staff could encourage Melissa to keep a diary of her bowel habits. In my experience the child is often more apt to talk or disclose information to an outside party than someone closer.'

Murmurs of agreement went off around the room each one slightly lower than the last like descending notes on a piano. I turned to look at Carol who was nodding in agreement; I had the feeling of being here before. I saw all the meetings I'd ever been at replayed, but I also knew this was the place to make a stand not only for Mel, but also for myself. I put up my hand.

'What if Mel doesn't respond? What's the plan?' I said it to them all but mainly I looked at Belinda and it was Belinda that answered.

'Why are you being so negative?' She flashed me a condescending smile.

I didn't like this woman. I felt it when I walked in the room the way she looked me over with narrow eyes. Her page-boy hair, her pink cheeks made it difficult to see if she was wearing any make up, but mostly they made it look like she was permanently angry. I clipped my words.

'I'm not being negative, I'm merely talking historically. In all this time Mel has refused, *declined* all treatment. Given that,' I felt Carol's eyes burning into me wanting me to shut up but I pushed on, 'I'm simply asking what if, even with your *professional* input, she doesn't comply? What's the back-up plan?'

Belinda's hands, which had been so still, began to slowly move and stretch in front of her like a cat sharpening its claws, but before she could answer Dr. Rayner interrupted.

'I think at present we have little choice but to allow Belinda the opportunity to move this forward. She has a vast amount of experience in matters like this and clearly, we will achieve nothing by forcing Melissa to attend the hospital even if it were an option.'

'For Christ's sake, Mel's a section 31. We're her corporate parent. We have a duty of care to take care of her,' I said.

Chairs shifted uncomfortably.

'Jerry, why don't you sit down?' said Carol, gently placing her hand on my arm.

I brushed it off. 'Mel was brought into care for reasons of neglect. Well, this,' I said, banging the table with my fist, 'what we're doing is neglect. If any of us in this room had a child with this problem and we allowed it to continue we would be done by Social Services for abuse. Well, on your own heads be it,' I spat the words. 'No. On Mel's head be it.' I sat down.

Someone poured a glass of water, a tiny ripple against the thickness of the silence that followed.

Arrangements were made for Belinda Marshal to contact Mel as soon as possible to put the plan into action. I expected a talking-to off Carol for my outburst but she said nothing. I didn't give a fuck I knew I'd done right.

*

I never remembered my dreams, but this one woke me. Vague images of white. A sterile, almost blinding room that made my eyes squint. A polished floor and a reek like burnt rubber mixed with something sickly. Blurred outlines of bodies standing huddled together, murmuring low, but I couldn't see or hear what they were saying.

I shouted out and pushed my way to the front but there was a tide of resistance in my legs, as if I was pulling a great weight. On a table was a new-born baby, in a foetal position. It floated before me like an apparition. I could hear it in my mind speaking but I couldn't tell what it was saying. The words were cloudy. There was no mouth and the child had a deformed head and large swollen eyes, deep black pools watching me.

I told Kate about the dream. She told me it was my subconscious mind stressed from work. She was right. I'd felt shut out from Mel's case, but why should I care? It was just a job and I was just a foot soldier.

I was in the kitchen making Mel a drink and took the opportunity to see how things were. 'How's it going with what's her name…Belinda?' It was a coy approach, a gentle prod.

'Fine,' said Mel taking a large gulp of orange juice. And then the bombshell came. 'Jerry, if a girl has her ovaries removed can she still have babies?'

I felt my heart jump. I was caught off guard, afraid in case I said the wrong thing. Mel looked at me, her eyes questioning. 'I'd just ask your doctor that one,' I said. 'I'm not sure.' The thought struck: why the fuck would a 13-year-old child ask such a thing? And then the dream came back.

*

'Do you mind if we fit supervision in, Jerry? It's been a while since you've had one,' asked Carol.

I hated supervision. It was all about targets and more fucking targets. I never had anything to say, it was just a fucking hoop you had to jump through to earn your daily bread. 'Yeah, no probs,' I said.

Carol came prepared. My supervision file was sitting on her desk as I followed into her office. She sat down making herself comfortable, turned the first few pages and peered at me over the rim of the file.

'Now, interaction with young people?' said Carol.

'Yeah I love them all,' I said sitting down.

Carol looked at me waiting for a little more, her pen poised.

'I get on with all the kids,' I added.

She scribbled down a few words and sat back. 'Practice issues?'

'None, I don't have a problem with anyone.'

She studied me for a moment.

I began doodling on a piece of paper in front of me.

'Jerry,' there was a tension to her voice and she hesitated before pushing on. 'Some of your colleagues,' she drew the word *colleagues* out, 'have commented that you're a little negative when you come into work.'

'What the fuck. Who said that?' I stood up giving her my full attention now. 'Tell you what, let them say it to my face, the spineless bastards.' I felt angry, hurt, people I thought were my friends whispering behind my back.

'Listen, I'm human, sometimes I'm happy and sometimes I'm sad, but as long as I do my job who cares?' I threw down my pen, might as well go all the way. 'So, who's come to you and said this? In fact tell them to say it to my face because they'll get both fucking barrels.'

The tone in Carol's voice took on an official quality, 'it's just what I've overheard, but if anyone had come to me then that's their right.'

'It might be their right, but I have a right to defend myself. People are so quick to judge, but has any one of my so called friends thought of coming to me and asking me if I'm okay? So much for the caring profession. Spineless bastards.'

Unsure how to push forward, Carol, gently tapped the end of her pen on the file in front of her. 'It's stuff like overtime, you don't do any. It's….' she searched for the right words, 'It's about supporting the team.'

'Supporting the team?' I couldn't believe what she'd said. 'You mean like they've just supported me?'

She looked flustered.

'I support one team and that's team Jerry and family. If there's a staff shortage that's not my problem, the powers that be should get their act together because while people cover the shifts things will never change. And just for the record Carol, it's called *overtime* it's not compulsory. Just because I'm not like fucking Margaret who phones in when she's off sick to tell the handyman that the toilet needs painting, doesn't make me not a team player, it makes her nuts. It's a job, a job.

' At least give me fucking credit for being honest, for having the guts to say what every other fucker thinks but won't say. I'm not going to end up like James. He gave his heart and soul to this place and what did it get him? A bunch of flowers from the bosses on high. And that was probably paid for out of petty cash and claimed back.' I stopped, aware I may have gone too far.

Carol stopped writing on the supervision sheet. There was nothing but the hum of the computer. It was no use arguing, I couldn't win. I decided to follow Matt's advice: 'Jerry,' he said, 'in this game you have to wear many hats. Play the game. Play the game.'

'Okay, what do you want me to do?' I asked in a calm gentle voice.

She was smiling now, once more comfortable in the moment. 'Be more positive, more upbeat, that's all.'

'Okay,' I said. She was right. I was negative. I was without purpose.

'There's one other thing.' She didn't make eye contact. Whatever she was about to tell me was not easy for her. 'We…I think it's best if Melissa has a female keyworker while she's going through this difficult time.'

'What?' I couldn't believe it. 'Why? What have I done wrong?' I was stunned.

'I think you're getting a little too involved and it's not good for you or Melissa.'

'Bollocks. For fuck's sake, they moan when you don't get involved and if you do,' my head was spinning now, 'and if you do, they take the kid off you.'

'Jerry it's not like that.'

'Wait a moment you said, *we* think it's for the best. Who are we? What's a matter, Carol, did I make all those so called professionals feel uncomfortable? Did one of their little foot soldiers have an original thought?'

'It's not like that.' Her eyes still didn't make contact. 'Lucy is to be allocated as Mel's new key worker.'

'No questions Lucy,' I smiled. 'That makes sense.'

*

Things went quiet for the next two weeks. I ambled along trying not to get uptight. I approached my work with a smile, a fake one, but nevertheless a smile. In those weeks calmness gathered over me, settling gently like freshly fallen snow and I began to feel unaffected by any concerns I'd had. Instead I felt secure in this new detachment I allowed myself. It was simply a game, a game of choice, the choice to wear your heart on your sleeve or the choice to conceal your thoughts and opinions.

I would often lie in bed thinking about my day. I'd be numb to the bad bits. The 'fuck offs', the threats to spit in my face and the contempt with which Leon spoke to me, all forgotten as I drifted into sleep. My detachment was short-lived.

*

I was in the office with Matt drinking coffee when there was a crash at the door. It was Terry, his eyes wide, his voice coming in gulps. 'It's Mel, she fell!' he yelled.

Mel was face down on the floor curled up tight as a spring in a foetal position. Matt looked to me.

'Ambulance,' I said.

Mel spat and snarled like a wild animal, as the paramedics attempted to lift her into the ambulance. In the end two police officers had to hold her down cuffing her. Eventually she was tamed not through reason but through force and exhaustion.

*

'Surgery?' Why? For what?'

I could see Carol's face, taut. She's wasn't sure how to approach the task in hand. It's funny how you learn people's rhythms; how you know when they're uncomfortable trying to convince themselves things are for the best.

'I can't tell you. It's confidential.'

I mirrored the words back, 'Confidential.' I bit my lip drawing blood.

'The main thing is,' said Carol, attempting to be diplomatic, 'she's going to be okay, at least now the problem's been dealt with.'

I surprised myself, I thought my anger would come in great waves, but instead there was only an exhausted, tiny echo of emotion.

*

On my way into work the next day an impulse took hold as I passed the hospital. I swung the car round. I took the steps two at a time. I pushed the buzzer and waited. A young nurse opened the door.

'I've come to see Mel— I'm her keyworker from Acorn house,' I said catching my breath.

The nurse took my request back and then returned with Belinda. Her eyes fixed me with authority as I watched her approach through the oblong glass in the security door.

'I've come to see Mel, I said.'

'I'm afraid you can't' see her, she's—'

'Fuck you.'

Belinda froze, opened her mouth to speak but I was already gone.

*

It was four weeks before Mel returned to Acorn Children's home. When she did she was frail but there was now some colour in her face and she no longer smelt. In all that time no member of staff was allowed to visit her, only Carol. Staff speculated amongst themselves.

'Cancer,' some said. 'Crohn's,' said others. 'No way, they would never let a kid… a child go through something like that, not for this long. Jerry, you know what's going on, you must know, you're just not saying that's all. You've been told to keep your mouth shut I bet.'

'Honest,' I said. 'I don't know.'

*

I came across it by sheer accident. Surprised no one else had. I was putting some work away in Mel's client diary when I saw the discharge information sheet. Blanked out at the top of the sheet in black felt tip marker, but detectable when held up to a strong light was the word, *Hysterectomy.* Why would a thirteen-year–old child have to have a hysterectomy? I showed it to Matt. Holding the paper against the light he let out a slow whistle.

'Doesn't surprise me at all,' he said. 'Best keep it under your hat.'

*

I was sitting at the kitchen table six-thirty in the morning. Kate had made me breakfast, smiling, a lightness in her manner that had been absent a long time. We both breathed it in, filled our bodies with it.

I left her packing Millie's lunch box and went out into the back garden. The morning light was shuffling in, gently pushing away the last of the darkness. A few slugs had climbed up the rainproof cover on the rabbit hutch; I flicked them off. The rabbits were a new addition, a present from me to Millie. She adored them.

The rabbit's twitching noses pushed against the mesh.

'Morning girls,' I said.

They hopped down the run to the bottom of the hutch and out onto the grass. I watched, as they stretched and then shook their bodies rejoicing in their freedom and began nibbling at the grass, their ears upright, rotating, listening.

*

Inside Kate had made more coffee. ‘Pass me the milk, hon,’ she said. There was a postcard stuck on the fridge door from the B&B we’d stayed at in Blackpool the weekend before, thanking us for our custom and inviting us to come again soon.

‘When did that come,’ I asked.

‘Yesterday.’

*

Early morning strolling down the beach in Blackpool, leaving Kate and Millie to sleep back at the B&B was when I’d come to my decision.

At that time of the day the air is clean and your thoughts flow easy, almost as if your head hasn’t had the time to fill up yet with all the worries of the day. I wondered how Mel’s life would pan out, what the future held for her. In front of me, on the sand, was a tiny fish flopping about, fighting for its life. Suddenly from out of nowhere I got to thinking how good it would be to beat the shit out of Leon and tie him to the beach and let the tide roll in, smothering his scummy little body forever. It wasn't a joke. At that moment I really could have done it. In that moment I knew it was time to quit the job.

I had begun, I believe, like most people; with the belief that one can and should strive to make a difference to the world in which they live and to help others. I was nevertheless, slowly worn away. It started gradually at first, little by little, like a light rainfall on a summer day, but just like a summer shower the sun always returned lifting my spirits and my hopes high, until finally, one day, the rainfall became a monsoon and no matter how hard I looked for the sunlight, it had disappeared.

I bent, picked the tiny life up and flung it back into the sea, a small act but a worthy one.

I went back to the B&B and woke Kate. I told her I was going to hand my notice in. She smiled, her eyes bright. 'We'll get by. You did your best, Jerry, no one could ask for more.'

'I'll find another job.'

'I know you will.'

Seeing Kate smiling and happy made my heart leap. I felt younger, reborn and free, like a man who'd just found out the doctors were wrong and his disease could be cured. I felt secure in whatever the future held.

*

I ate the last of my toast, finished up my coffee and put on my coat.

'You all set?' asked Kate.

I let out a long sigh. 'You bet.'

She kissed me full on the lips then hugged me real hard. 'Enjoy it,' she said laughing. 'It's your last day. You're free.'

I hugged her back.

'Got your letter?'

I patted my breast pocket. 'Oh yes.'

*

Matt was in the kitchen when I got to work.

'Morning, Jerry, want a cuppa?'

I went over to the cupboard and passed him a cup. 'How was last night?' I asked.

'Same shit different bucket.' He poured the tea and handed me one. He studied me over the rim of his cup for a moment. I must have worn my joy like a neon sign because he asked. 'What's on your mind, Jerry?'

I sipped my tea and shook my head. 'Nothing. Why?'

He looked me up and down, searching for a clue. 'Fuck me, Jerry, you've won the lottery.'

I let out a big laugh. 'No. But you're right; there is something I want to tell you.'

'You're not gay are you?'

'Matt, be serious.'

Matt's face took on a solemn look.

'I'm leaving, today, after my shift.'

Matt puffed out his cheeks. 'Leaving? Bollocks.' He put down his cup. 'Why? I mean when did this happen? Why?'

'It's lots of things, Mel, Leon, the fact that we never change or alter anything.'

'So what? Just take the money and forget about it.' Matt pulled at the end of his beard. 'What will you do for money?'

'I've got a little saved and Kate can pick up a few extra hours at work just until I find something, anything.'

There was nothing but the click of the refrigerator as it regulated its temperature.

'You'll need to give notice.'

'We'll see.'

Matt thoughtfully sipped at his tea. 'Well, I guess congratulations are in order,' he said smiling. 'What time you telling Carol?'

'At the end of the shift.'

Matt rolled his eyes. 'Good luck with that.' Then in a serious tone, 'She'll be sad to see you go.'

'Perhaps.'

'To tell you the truth, I don't think I'll be far behind you.'

Somehow I knew Matt would never leave. He was comfortable. He could handle it. He expected not to make a difference and accepted it without any concern.

'You will stay in touch?' he asked.

'Behave. Of course I will.'

I held out my hand, he took it and pulled me into a hard embrace. There was a bang at the door and an inaudible shout. Leon's face was pressed against the glass. I shot a glance at the clock. 'What's he doing up so early?'

'His mother gets her benefits today. He wants to catch her early so he can get some cigs.'

'What do you want Leon?' I asked through the glass.

I opened the door to be greeted by Leon laughing. 'What you two wankers doing? Kissing?'

'What do you want?' asked Matt in a weary tone.

Leon looked round the kitchen then opened the fridge door. 'Some bacon.'

I looked to Matt.

'Cooks not in till nine,' said Matt.

Leon's chest swelled up, his face tightened.

'I'll cook it,' I said. 'But only when you're out the kitchen.'

*

Leon plunged into his bacon on toast, ripping it to shreds and stuffing it into his tiny mouth. I sat opposite him and watched as he parted his bread to administer a large helping of tomato sauce. Pleased with the results he took a bite and wiped his mouth with the back of his sleeve, snorting as he did so.

I straightened a table mat and adjusted the corner of the table cloth.

'So tell me, Leon, what's your hopes and dreams for the future?'

He looked up, his mouth widening into a grin, his teeth jostled for position. 'Go on benefits like me Mum.'

That ended our little chat. I sat and watched as he finished off his breakfast, then he let out a deafening burp before taking a large gulp of milk. He then proceeded to stick his little finger up his nose. He pulled out a large crow and wiped it on the tablecloth.

'Leon, that's disgusting.'

He shrugged and rubbed at his nose. As he got up he caused the table to shift knocking over what was left of his milk.

'You might want to clean that up,' I said.

'You clean it up,' he sniffed. 'That's what you get paid for.'

He moved past me towards the office door. 'Matt, give us some travel money,' he shouted.

Matt's voice came back. 'No chance mate, you should be at your educational placement.'

'Twat,' shouted Leon kicking at the office door. He calmly turned towards me. 'Jerry, lend us three quid.'

'I can't, you know that.'

He kicked at the office door again. 'Matt, can I use the phone then?'

The door opened.

'Who you phoning?'

'Me Mum.'

Matt held out the phone. 'Bring it back when you finish.'

Leon shot up the stairs.

*

I opened the diary to see what we had on for the day.

'Matt, it says here Leon's social worker is visiting him at ten.'

Matt took hold of the diary. 'You better phone and tell him Leon's off out. Save him the journey.'

I placed the phone to my ear and was about to dial only to hear the clipped upper class accent of a woman speaking. For a moment I was unsure, as to why some woman would be on the line. Then

I remembered Leon was on the line phoning his mum. I was even more surprised as to how posh his mother spoke. Then the woman's words began to filter through. *'I've been a bad girl. Do you want me to suck your cock?'*

I cupped my hand over the receiver and motioned for Matt to listen. We both burst into laughter.

'It's one of those sex lines,' Matt whispered. 'He must be having a tug before he goes out.'

We listened a few moments longer to the posh lady describe how she wanted Leon to punish her, both of us shaking with muffled laughter. I gently placed the receiver down. 'I wonder how long he's been doing that?' I said. 'No wonder the phone bill comes in on a toilet roll.'

Five minutes later Leon appeared at the door.

'You looked flushed, Leon. You okay?' I said.

Matt started laughing.

'What's so funny?' said Leon, handing Matt the phone.

'I don't want it. Give it to him,' said Matt shooting me a smile.

'What's so funny?'

'Nothing, Jerry just told me a joke.'

I held the phone between my thumb and index finger and dropped it on the desk.

Leon looked at me, shaking his head. 'You're weird. Right I'm off.'

I followed Leon out into the hall. He turned towards me and pulled a bus pass from his pocket.

'Where'd you get that?'

Leon tapped his finger to his nose. 'Not for you to know.'

I edged closer, trying to see if it had the correct date on it or if it was an old one but Leon hugged it to his chest.

'You wanner see?'

'Sure,' I said, inching forward.

He held it out. 'FOD!' The heel of his hand struck my forehead.

You little cunt, I thought. I raised my hand with the full intention of striking him back. I mean *what the hell it was my last day.*

Leon rose up on the balls of his feet. 'Go on,' he hissed. 'I'll get you done.'

I swallowed hard, regaining my composure.

Leon's face broke into a beaming smile. 'You know, Jerry, I was thinking, I could get any member of staff the sack.' He licked his lips, his tongue flicking out like a stalking lizard. 'I mean, if I made an allegation they would believe me. They always believe kids over staff.'

I smiled. 'There was me thinking, poor little child in care.'

Leon sniffed, put his hand in his pocket. 'I found something for you, Jerry,' he said, taking his hand out and holding up his middle finger.

We both turned at the sound of the front door opening. Carol stepped in.

'Morning, Leon. Morning, Jerry. You're looking bright today, Leon. Hope you're being a good boy.'

'I am, Carol, I am.' Leon's eyes glowed. 'Can I have some travel money please, Carol?'

***

Chapter 24

I think Carol knew it was coming, the way she held the crisp white envelope in her hand, turning it over like an unwanted gift.

'It's my resignation. I've not given the customary four weeks' notice,' I said. 'I'm going today and if they don't like it they can go and...well you get the idea.'

'I know. Sit down, Jerry.' She placed the envelope on her desk, standing it upright like an ivory-coloured gravestone. 'Jerry, have you thought this through, what you're giving up?'

I gave her an enquiring look.

'Your pension and all the benefits of working for a local authority.'

I slowly shook my head, after all this time she didn't get it. 'It's not about that, Carol. It's about saving my soul before it's too late.'

A smile broke across her face and I knew she was thinking, same old Jerry, thinking too much. 'I understand,' she said. 'I do understand. What will you do?'

'I really don't know. Perhaps I'll be a postman.'

Carol raised a disbelieving eyebrow.

'Well it beats walking the streets,' I said. A small trickle of laughter escaped from Carol and for a moment we were caught up in the niceness of it all.

'Can I change your mind?'

I looked around at the walls, at the pictures of kids that had passed through Acorn House, lined up like smiling statistics next to a memo from the resource manager praising the latest OFSTED report, next to another memo relating to the number of staff illnesses.

'Carol, what do we achieve? What do *they* achieve?' I asked, pointing at the pictures. 'You tell me one of those kids that have gone on to be anything but a casualty of care, a fucking statistic?'

Carol made no attempt to offer a defence. She was going to take her beating.

'The system gives them money like candy. Everything revolves around money: You give them laptops for education, they sell them for drugs. Any kid that comes to , within a week refuses school and within two is doing pot and whatever else they can get their hands on. And there's nothing, *nothing* we can do about it.'

It spewed out of me like a severed artery: The myth of short- term placements and how once a kid is put in care that's it until they're sixteen or seventeen.

'Activities everyday: bowling, cinema, go-carting, holidays. It's like fucking Centre Parcs. What family can compete with that?' As I spoke each outburst fed the next, fuelling it, giving it fire.

'We have young girls that prostitute themselves and we have absolutely no power to stop them because it's *their choice.*'

'We teach them to respect *nothing.* If a kid makes an allegation, physical or sexual, for a laugh, it's the member of staff who suffers. There's no apology, no consequence to their action. Fuck me, there's no consequence to anything.'

Throughout my tirade of venting, cleansing anger, Carol never made a sound. She just blinked, as if the light was hurting her eyes.

I took a deep breath and collapsed into the chair spent. When next I spoke my voice was almost a whisper, a call to reason. 'What do we do Carol? What do we *really* do? We produce thugs and future thugs, prison fodder.'

Carol made a small gesture with her hand as if she was about to interrupt, voice a defence.

'Carol, don't. Please don't. You know I'm right.' I let out a half-hearted laugh at the ridiculousness of it all. For a moment there was silence between us. Then in a hushed voice I said,' 'I need to know the truth about Mel.'

Carol shook her head. 'I can't discuss that. It's confidential and against procedures.'

'Oh come on, we all know that she had a hysterectomy.'

Carol looked genuinely surprised.

'It was written on her discharge note, we've all seen it. The question is why? For Christ's sake, I'm as good as gone,' I said pointing to the envelope. 'What difference does it make?'

'Is that what this is all about?'

Carol bit down on her bottom lip. This was a big decision for her. She got up and took a moment, took a deep breath. When she spoke her voice was low and nervous. 'Don't mention this to anyone because if you do, I'll deny all knowledge.'

'Mel had…well she had a hysterectomy. She had a sexually transmitted disease.' She let out a heavy breath, 'Gonorrhoea.' She said the word like she'd put something unpleasant into her mouth. 'It caused a problem in her fallopian tubes necessitating…well the correct medical term is a radical hysterectomy. Even I don't know *all* the details.'

She was like a train now, picking up speed, pushing ahead. I let her run. Perhaps she needed to tell someone, anyone.

'We do know that, at some point, Melissa had a miscarriage without telling anyone. The general thinking is the mother's partner abused her, but Melissa wouldn't say who she'd slept with.'

'Jesus, Carol, what the fuck.'

'Probably thought it was betraying her mother if she told. Perhaps she thought it would prevent her ever returning home. Maybe she thought her mother wouldn't believe her and choose the partner over her.'

Carol shrugged her shoulders. 'No one but Melissa knows for sure. In the end she only agreed to treatment if we asked no questions and didn't tell her mother any of the details.'

I sat with my head lowered, a sadness descended over me. I dug my palms deep into my eye sockets trying to rub away the feeling. 'What if it hadn't taken eight, nine months to treat her? Then what? Would things have been different? I mean she'll never be able to have children.'

'I know.'

The words came out, low and barely audible. It was as close to an admission of the whole fucking charade I was going to get, but then Carol straightened, regained her composure. 'The right decision was taken. It had to be Melissa's choice. Anything else would have been an infringement upon her rights.'

'The right decision; are you fucking blind?'

Carol's face hardened. 'Now wait a minute,' she said hurt.

I cut her short. 'No, you wait.' In that moment Carol looked frail and withered, as if to move would shatter her into a thousand pieces. I looked her straight in the eyes. 'Say it anyway you want but because of us that girl will never know what it's like to be a mother. If that was my kid, your kid we would have sorted it months ago and not let it run on and on.' I let out a tiny sarcastic laugh. 'They talk about protecting children from adults, but they can't even protect children from themselves.'

I stood up.

'I'm leaving. I need to be out in the light before it's too late.'

As I got to the door Carol's hand reached out and touched mine. 'I'm sorry."

I gently squeezed her hand. 'I know. I am too.'

*

The door clicked shut behind me and for a moment I stood still, my heart pounding. Poor Carol had taken the full hit. Poor Carol, making a living being the acceptable face of an unacceptable system.

Epilogue.

Outside, Leon was smoking. For a long time I sat in the car and watched as he stepped on and off the step, spitting first on the floor, then on the glass of the door and then launching his whole body behind the spit, seeing how far he could make it go. This was it, I was truly free. This would be the final time I would drive away from Acorn House. I felt like I should shout out; yell, 'I've escaped,' but I was struck silent by the wonder of it all.

I wound the window down.

'Hey, Leon, come here a min.'

Leon raised his middle finger to me before cupping his hands around his cigarette, relighting it, protecting it from the wind. He shuffled towards me, sniffed.

'Wah?'

I flashed him a smile. I wanted to tell Leon of my freedom, communicate it to him in a way he would understand but as I looked at him standing there, one hand holding his cigarette the other down the front of his tracky bottoms, *why waste your energy,* I thought. He wouldn't understand. He wouldn't give a shit. 'Take care of yourself, Leon,' I said dismissing him with a wave of my hand.

'Whatever,' he turned and started to walk away.

'Hey, Leon, one more thing.'

'What's that?' he sniffed.

I stepped out the car.

Leon's eyes grew wide and his mouth opened into a grin. He coughed up phlegm and spat it onto the pavement just missing my shoe.

'I've got something for you, Leon.'

'What's that?'

I smiled and with all my hate and all my anger, I said, 'Just this, Leon.' I took the palm of my hand and with a joy and a calmness that surprised me, I announced my freedom.

'FOD!'

Approximately 6000 children per year emerge from the care system. Within two years:

3000 will be unemployed.
2,100 will be mothers or pregnant.
1,200 will be homeless.
4,500 will leave care with no qualifications.
60 will make it to University.
80% of Big Issue sellers have been through the care system.

It is theorised that a successful system of care would transform the country:

. It would empty one-third of our prisons.
. It would shift half of all prisoners under the age of 25 and of the criminal justice system.
.It would halve the number of prostitutes.
. It would reduce between one-third and one half, the number of homeless people.

Acknowledgements

I'd like to thank members of Skelmersdale Writers' Group for all their support. I am also indebted to Amanda Richardson for her tell it like it is honest criticism. A special thanks to the author, Carol Fenlon for more proofreading and suggestions. Thank you to my lovely children for loving their Dad.
Thanks to Elizabeth Brown for her help in preparing this book for publication.
Finally, gratitude and respect to Dr J. Alexander, Dr M Schulz, Ann Strong, Hilary Morgan, Surgeon, Mr. A. Sharma and all the staff at the Royal Liverpool Hospital for everything you do and continue to do. Long live the NHS.

***

Lightning Source UK Ltd.
Milton Keynes UK
UKHW040837100219
337025UK00001B/202/P